DIVINING ROD

Also by Michael Knight

Dogfight and Other Stories

DIVINING

ROD

Michael Knight

A DUTTON BOOK

DUTTON
Published by the Penguin Group
Penguin Putnam Inc., 375 Hudson Street, New York, New York 10014, U.S.A.
Penguin Books Ltd, 27 Wrights Lane, London W8 5TZ, England
Penguin Books Australia Ltd, Ringwood, Victoria, Australia
Penguin Books Canada Ltd, 10 Alcorn Avenue, Toronto, Ontario, Canada M4V 3B2
Penguin Books (N.Z.) Ltd, 182–190 Wairau Road, Auckland 10, New Zealand

Penguin Books Ltd, Registered Offices: Harmondsworth, Middlesex, England

First published by Dutton, an imprint of Dutton NAL,
a member of Penguin Putnam Inc.

First Printing, October, 1998

10 9 8 7 6 5 4 3 2 1

Grateful acknowledgment is made for permission to reprint an excerpt from "Looking Forward to Age" from *The Theory and Practice of Rivers* by Jim Harrison, Clark City Press, 1989. By permission of the publisher.

REGISTERED TRADEMARK—MARCA REGISTRADA

LIBRARY OF CONGRESS CATALOGING-IN-PUBLICATION DATA:
Knight, Michael.
    Divining rod / by Michael Knight.
        p. cm.
    ISBN 0-525-94379-X
    I. Title.
PS3561.N486D58 1998
813'.54—dc21   98-15445
                                                              CIP

Printed in the United States of America
Set in Palatino

PUBLISHER'S NOTE
This is a work of fiction. Names, characters, places, and incidents either are the product of the author's imagination or are used fictitiously, and any resemblance to actual persons, living or dead, events, or locales is entirely coincidental.

This book is printed on acid-free paper.

For Jill

ACKNOWLEDGMENTS

First and foremost thanks to Warren Frazier, who has invested more in this book than any right-thinking person otherwise would have. Thanks also to Jennifer Dickerson, my editor, and to Meg Tipper and all the Gilman crew for much time and support. To the folks at Hollins College for helping support this nasty writing habit, and a special I-could-not-have-done-it-without-you to a certain bibliophile who shall remain nameless at this time.

Part I

To walk in ruins, like vain ghosts, we love,
And with fond divining wands
We search among the dead
For treasure buried
While the liberal earth does hold
So many virgin mines of undiscovered gold.

—Abraham Cowley

How It Ended

Sam Holladay was sixty-three years old when he jabbed a
snub-nosed .38 revolver into Simon Bell's chest and pulled
the trigger, knocking him flat, like he'd been shoved, and
dead, the bullet passing through his heart and exiting at his
left shoulder, trailing blood and tissue like the tail of a com-
et. It was a July Sunday. It was late morning, long pine shadows drawn on the flat ground. Bell had, the day before, driven
a riding mower over the lawn so the air smelled of cut grass
and the clippings stuck to the men's shoes and clung to Bell's
hair, where he lay on the ground. Sam Holladay stood over
him a moment, then went into Bell's house and called the police himself.

He had expected to have to face some sort of consequence
right off, but the house was quiet and empty. He'd been
there before, years ago, and the place still looked the same to
him. All the furniture exactly as he remembered it, the same
pictures on the mantel. He let himself wander back to the
bedroom and sat on the edge of the mattress, his forearms
across his knees. He made the call, then went into the kitchen

for a glass of water. The sink was a clutter of crusted dishes, a week's worth at least, piled precariously to the edge. When he leaned his face close to wet his fingers and dab his eyelids with cool water, he could smell the faint, damp thickness of rot. A few empty beer bottles on the counter, like glass skyscrapers of a model city. A pot of coffee burned to carbon. He tried to think of his wife, closed his eyes and imagined her in another kitchen, their kitchen, not twenty yards away, pictured her taking copper pots from their hooks on the wall and arranging them on the stove. She was, he knew, making breakfast. He wondered if she'd heard the shot—she played the radio too loud when she cooked—if, just for an instant, she'd turned away from the stove to look in the direction of the report. He didn't know what would happen now, what events would follow, but he worried about her. Through the window above the sink, Holladay could make out Simon Bell's body, just a shape in the grass, no more ominous or frightening than a dress shop mannequin.

Simon Bell

My father bought the house on Speaking Pines Road and all the furniture in one ridiculous and sweeping impulse the day after he proposed to my mother. He was so thrilled that she said yes, he found a realtor, scrawled out a check for the down payment, then hurried all over lower Alabama buying couches and end tables, armoires and love seats, without regard to interior space or a coherent design scheme. Finally, standing in line to buy a beanbag chair in a head shop stocked with dope-smoking paraphernalia from a guy with stringy hair and a half-assed goatee who would have ordinarily sent my father off on a tirade, his credit card was rejected, and he came reeling to his senses.

Being a stubborn man and generally a financial pragmatist, my father would neither admit that the house looked absurd nor part with the money needed to replace the furniture. I could imagine the first time my parents saw the place together, the two of them standing in the living room, turning slow, dazed circles, my mother wondering what she'd gotten herself into and trying to think of a tactful way to suggest a few changes, and my father boiling with humiliation but keeping a straight face, refusing to admit his mistake. He was not a man who liked to say that he was wrong.

He did all right on the house itself—redbrick Georgian, four bedrooms, two and a half baths, across from a golf course, zero crime rate. My father was forty-nine when he married my mother, fifty-two when they had me. He'd been a bachelor for so long that he never really got the hang of domesticity. And my mother was a trooper until his death, subtle and determined. Over the years, she picked up new pieces of furniture, slipped them into the house one at a time, so my father hardly noticed that the house was looking less preposterous.

He died when I was home on summer vacation from college. It was just after five o'clock and swallows flitted in the trees. My father was soaking himself in the swimming pool behind the house, his head tilted back, eyes closed, elbows up on the deck, and my mother was inside playing records for him, music trickling through the open windows. I was sitting in the patio doorway, exactly halfway between them. It was nice to be home for a while, the daylight blurring, the birds chanting arcanely. The phone rang, and I went inside to answer it, so that neither of them would be disturbed, and when I returned, my father was dead. He had climbed out of the pool, maybe to tell someone about the pain in his chest, and I found him on his side with his knees drawn up, his mouth open like a sleeping child.

To my amazement, I found that I couldn't muster sadness. I wanted to be in agony, like my mother, shattered and useless, feeling his absence in my body like a wound, but, more than anything else, his death had left me stunned and blank.

I presided over the funeral in a sort of bewildered haze. The service was held at graveside, the crowd wilting in the late August simmer. Folding metal chairs were set out beneath a striped funeral parlor tent. Afterward, I had no recollection of my eulogy or of the warm, consoling hands of mourners or even of my mother in the front row, paralyzed with anguish. What I remembered most vividly was the sight of his secretaries, six of them, seated all in a row, sharing handkerchiefs, shaking with sobs, like the bereaved widows of a polygamist king.

My father, the original Simon Bell, founder, owner, and operator of Bell Tractor & Machine. He had a team of secretaries, each one more homely than the next, his outer office a showcase of dowdy middle-aged proficiency, women who didn't do anything that I could tell. A procession of sprawling midsections and terrifyingly wide behinds, of pancake makeup and witches' hair, as if to imply by the unattractiveness of these women that his operation was strictly business.

When I was a boy, I was convinced he did every job at the company. His coarse, oil-slicked hands turned each bolt and nut on every tractor. I saw him working the showroom. I pictured him driving hump-backed transport rigs loaded with combines and backhoes and bulldozers to Bell distributors in other cities. The bulldozers were my favorite. Mother and I would pass a highway crew when she was driving me to school, the bulldozer scooping away pavement like ice cream, and I would swivel around in my seat, thinking my father was in the cockpit. She never told me I was wrong.

Once, late at night, he took me with him to the manufacturing warehouse of Bell Tractor to crash an illicit meeting. His employees were trying to form a union. My father stood on the hood of one of his tractors, a tractor he had invented using the knowledge of machines that he'd picked up as a tank mechanic in the army. I was nine years old. He lifted me up to stand in front of him, holding my shoulders firmly, so I couldn't turn away from the crowd of workmen. He told everyone to take a look at me, to get a good look. If I hear any more rumblings about a union, he said, I will sell off every last piece of machinery, every last square foot of land that the machinery is sitting on, and give the proceeds to this boy, my son. He and his family will be taken care of for generations and you, gentlemen, will be out of a job.

That was that, or at least as well as I remember it. All of those pairs of eyes on me. My father stalked out, pushing me along ahead of him, the crowd breaking up around him as if he were surrounded by a force field. That's the way I imagined his life, when he'd finished his morning coffee and left my mother and me standing on the front porch. Even after I was old enough to know better. All of the people around him seemed unnecessary. It was impossible that he was dead. I kept expecting to come downstairs, in the days that followed his funeral, and find him at the kitchen table reading the paper and waiting for his breakfast, steam rising from a coffee mug in his hand.

I spent the rest of that summer pretending to be in misery. I went around the house heaving great, heartbreaking sighs. I'd stand in the front door, glance longingly over my shoulder, and announce that I was going for a drive, as if a lonely drive might be just the thing to get me back on my feet. I was terrified someone would discover I wasn't wretched with loss.

During the day, I swatted a golf ball around the neighborhood course, thirty-six holes at a time. At night, I drank beer, chased girls I didn't know. I couldn't bear to be in the house, couldn't stand the sight of my mother, tired-eyed and beautiful with sorrow. I told my friends that I was staying home to keep an eye on my poor mother, told my mother I was out with my friends. I had a secret week-long romance with a Puerto Rican woman named Pilar who bought me beer because I was underaged. When she said my name, it came out long and whiny, and I liked the way it sounded on her voice. Like I was someone different than myself. "Seemone," she'd say, "Keez me, Seemone."

I'd sleep awhile with my head on her shoulder before going home.

She said, "Your papa is dead, Seemone. How come you are here with me and not with you madre?"

"I love you," I said.

She thought that was funny. She laughed and stroked my head and said, "You should be at home. Not in love with me."

When fall finally came, I went back to school, and my mother started seeing a fortune teller. She drove halfway across town to consult a woman who dispensed mystic wisdom at her kitchen table, her crystal ball beside a jug of grocery store wine. My mother said she never wanted to be caught off guard again. She sent me long letters full of ridiculous prophecy. Don't ride in a long white car, Simon. Whatever you do, avoid red-headed women who drink gin. I figured she'd snap out of it after a little while. In those days, every moon was full of portent for her, every drifting hawk a harbinger.

There was a terrific picture of her on the mantel. My father took the shot with their first color camera, the image grainy, the tones sepia and blurred. She was sitting on the hood of their car, a 1959 DeSoto Firesweep convertible, long and elegant, stretching away in the picture to angled fins. She was twenty-eight, my age, married just a few weeks to a man more than twenty years her senior, and she was beautiful in a quiet way, her hair pressed down with a yellow scarf, a dark ring of it spilling onto her forehead, her eyes hidden behind cat's eye sunglasses. Her arms were spread in a gesture of embrace, her feet propped, toes pointing down, on the bumper. A young wife on a new car, her proud smile frozen in time with a brand-new camera.

My mother was a lover of horror movies, the bloodier the better. She would study the *TV Guide* for weeks, looking for just the right picture, then make my father watch with her, the two of them sitting on the couch, my mother squealing with delight, my father stiff and unamused. He said he had no desire to suspend his disbelief for that sort of feebleminded waste of film. But gradually, as my mother became more and more afraid, his hand would creep along the back of the couch until she was tucked firmly beneath his arm.

She liked to hide in closets or behind doors and leap out at my father or me when we least expected it. Just to get the blood going, she'd say. It's good for you to be afraid once in a while. My father always kept his composure, pretended that she hadn't scared him, but one time when he was coming in from work, after what I guessed was a particularly trying day, she sprang out from behind the living room curtains and grabbed his shoulders. On instinct, he turned and cold-cocked her, sent her sprawling over the coffee table, scattering magazines like startled quail, breaking a porcelain lamp that she loved. I heard all the commotion and came hustling out from my room. I saw the lamp first, the pieces like chips of bone. My father was cradling her, her head on his shoulder, a trickle of blood running from her nose. Both of them were crying. I'd never seen my father cry before. I didn't know what had happened, but I knew it must have been something terrible, so I wedged myself in between them and let the tears fly. We stayed like that, weeping in a strange, almost happy way, like a bankrupt farmer who'd won the lottery too late to save the family land.

Exactly six months from the day of my father's death, my mother drowned in the Gulf of Mexico. Her body washed ashore, pale and bloated, about a half mile down the beach from a house that she had rented. And I was home again, conferring her body to the ground. There were rumors that she had committed suicide, walked into the water, let it fill her lungs. But I didn't believe that sort of talk. No one died from loneliness or a broken heart anymore. I knew that. A few days after her funeral, I filled the bathtub—a clawfooted leftover from my father's shopping spree—with warm water, drank seventeen beers, and held my head under for as long as I could. As miserable as I wanted to be, I only lasted a minute and a half.

The first time I saw Delia Holladay, she helped me unload my car. I was moving back into my parents' house. This was the tail end of April, seven years after my mother's death, the air already rich with summer. Delia crossed the driveway from next door and introduced herself. She had a broad, scrubbed-looking country girl's face and round hips and green eyes. When she shook my hand, she looked down at her bare feet, curled her toes into the grass.

11

I said, "I didn't know Sam had children."

She looked at me a moment, her eyes pleating at the corners to pinch out the sun. A wisp of corn-yellow hair was caught at the corner of her mouth. My car was still ticking from the heat. She hauled a duffel bag from the trunk, her arms slender and tan, and said, "I'm his wife. Almost a year now."

"Shit," I said. "Sorry."

She laughed and let the duffel fall at her feet and crossed her arms. "Don't feel bad," she said. "People think that way all the time."

It only took us three trips to get my belongings inside. I didn't have much that was my own, a few suitcases and a golf bag and a lamp that had been given to me by a girl I wanted to remember, the meager accumulations of my life so far. Before she left the house, Delia asked what I'd been doing since I moved away. She said she'd always felt strange having an empty house next door. I didn't know what to tell her. Standing in the open doorway, an air-conditioned breeze wafting out, drying the sweat on my back, I couldn't, for a few seconds, remember how I had been living my life. It was as if I'd been stricken suddenly with complete amnesia. I tried a smile. I said, "Oh, you know. Nothing really."

When she was gone, I stretched out on the couch, a vague uneasiness swimming over me, and made a mental list of all the things that I had done. I went back to college after my mother died, then to law school, because everyone was going to law school in those days, then a year in the trust department of a bank in Mobile. I slept and ate dinner and watched television, like everybody else. I had my teeth cleaned on occasion and I went to parties. There must have been some parties sometime. I remembered reading a book, a mystery, and buying a Christmas present for the office secretary, this magazine rack made of wicker. There was a place I'd go for drinks after work, where the bartender came to recognize me but never knew my name. I bought new suits. Once, I cooked breakfast for a Jehovah's Witness. She showed up at my apartment, all clear skin and good intentions. She was maybe eighteen, so I let her in. I'd been reading financial reports at the kitchen table, and I shoved them aside so she could have room for her brochures. I put bacon strips in the microwave, got some bread going in the toaster. Her teeth were white as windowsills.

My Jehovah's Witness covered my hand with hers and told me in sincere tones about the Kingdom of Heaven—verdant fields, man and beast living together in harmony, all pictured in full-color newsprint. She kept pausing and looking at me, blinking her eyes like she was surprised that I hadn't yet chased her away. It was the longest, most pleasant conversation I'd had in months. Light was streaming through the windows and getting mixed up in her hair. When she asked me to give myself up to the Lord, I closed my eyes, leaned across the table, and kissed her on the mouth. I felt her lips go rigid beneath mine. When I opened my eyes, she was looking at me with such candid, sorrowful disappointment, her eyes the watery amber of riverbed stones, I would have given anything in the world for a better heart.

I spent my childhood in Sherwood, Alabama. The town was spread out along the Arrowhead River, hemmed in by piney woods and red clay bluffs. There was a paper mill and Bell Tractor and a community college, work enough for six thousand men and women. It was a county seat, so there was a courthouse downtown, one of those white-washed beauties that you couldn't find anymore. The day after my disaster with the Jehovah's Witness, I sent letters to all three law firms in Sherwood and, to my surprise, one of them accepted my application.

The house was quiet when I returned, full of echoes and ghosts, but I got the pool cleaned up, the appliances running. The firm worked me to death most days, doing legwork and research for more senior attorneys, but I managed to sneak away from the office a few evenings a week and stretch out on a deck chair beside the pool. I liked to listen to the voices of lady golfers drifting over my fence. That seemed to me a deep and wonderful thing. The breeze ruffling the surface of the water, the grand evening shadows and those secret phrases in the air. Sometimes my neighbor, Bob Robinson, would be playing with his kids on their side of the fence. One dog or another was always barking down the street. It was one of those neighborhoods. Everybody owned an acre or two of simple pleasures. And the lady golfers—their voices were like memories of real speech, faint and easy, no more troubled than the day's last light sifting down through the branches of the trees.

Summer was the busy season for attorneys. The air went heavy and damp and sound seemed to carry farther, the way it did underwater; the incessant ringing of insects, the machine rumble of traffic and construction, the earth itself coming to life again, greenery pushing in on highways, lawns refusing to stay mown. The days went on too long for you to fill them. You could taste the summer in Alabama, like walking into a room full of pipe smoke and breath and the closeness of bodies. It either tried your patience or made you languid and lazy in a way that I could understand.

My work was mostly civil, disputes between parties, generally resolved by a financial settlement, but the season had its effect on the non-criminal courts as well. There were more divorces filed in summer, for example, the heat wearing couples out, and more inheritance disputes. There was even a rise in complaints about loud music and dogs barking late into the night—animals, too, registered the change—simple things, ordinarily hashed out between reasonable people.

The second time I spoke to Delia Holladay, she came by to ask if she could use the pool. She was wearing a black one-piece swimsuit, a towel wrapped at her waist. I looked forward to those undisturbed afternoons, lounging with my lady golfers, but I didn't see how I could refuse. Her hair was piled on top of her head, like magic, suspended there without any sort of device that I could see. I led her through the house, told her I had some things to take care of, then slipped upstairs and watched her from the window of my parents' room—her toes-out walk across the flagstones, her hesitation at the edge of the pool, letting the towel trail behind her like a cape. She visited almost every evening and I moved a little closer each time, ducking out to see if she wanted something to drink the next day, then standing on the patio for a few minutes exchanging pleasantries the day after that, her hair slick against her skull, her arms and breasts buoyed by the water in the shallow end. Finally, in my deck chair, while she swam laps, cutting a path through clear water.

One day, I watched her climb the ladder, water streaming over her hips and legs, watched her shake the water from her hair with her fingers. I didn't notice that she was aware of my staring, until she waved a hand across the line of my gaze and said, "You've never seen a woman in a bathing suit before?"

"My father died right where you're standing," I said.

She stood looking at me for a few seconds, her eyes going soft, then crossed the patio and rested her hand on the top of my head for an instant before going home. I hadn't intended to tell her about my father, hadn't even known that he was on my mind, until I said the words aloud. For three days, Delia didn't show. I sat out by the pool alone, nursing a drink. The lady golfers chattered and chimed. Then Friday, hurrying home just in case, I found her walking up the street with a golf bag slung over one shoulder, her hair tied back in a ponytail. I stopped the car and rolled down the window to say hello. She waved and hesitated, then crossed her arms on the doorframe, rested her chin on the backs of her hands.

"You haven't been swimming," I said.

"I'm teaching myself to play golf," she said. "How hard could it be? All those old ladies out there."

"I used to play this course all the time."

"Maybe you'll give me a lesson one day," she said. "Sam promised to teach me, but he has conveniently let it slip his mind."

She grinned and adjusted the padded strap on her shoulder and walked off toward the first tee, her spikes ticking on the asphalt, the bag bumping against her hip. I sat there for a minute looking at the long row of houses. The place looked unfamiliar to me all of a sudden. I was on my street. I was sitting in my car. The sky was lazy with sunlight. I'd had the car detailed the day before and could smell the chemical odor of cleaning agent and the faintest trace of Delia's perfume and shampoo and whatever else it was that made women smell the way they do. I had a distinct, dreamy sensation of lingering movement, as if my blood had changed direction on me. Before I knew what I was doing, I'd parked the car and hurried over to the course to watch her.

Delia's stroke was something to see. Her chin tucked down, her shoulders sweeping around smoothly, her hand coming up to shade her eyes. Despite all that, she couldn't hit a decent shot to save her life. She topped the ball with her driver, sending it dribbling a few yards from the tee. She managed both a slice and a hook from the fairway, the direction of the ball as unpredictable as gambling dice. Her chips were invariably too long, her putting abysmal. Every now and then, she'd lift the tail of her shirt, absently, to wipe her face, exposing her belly button and the breathtaking curve of her rib cage.

She played every Monday, Wednesday, and Friday, always alone, always close to dusk when night was beginning to take the edge off of the heat. I was around for the first hole, hiding among the unused golf carts, and I was there at eighteen, when she would tally her scorecard in white ankle socks and saddle shoes. I kept to the rough, crouched among the young, sappy pines and fragrant dogwoods. She launched dozens of unwary balls into the woods, sending me scrambling for safety. I would press myself against the ground when she came in looking for them and pray that she didn't find me instead.

"Here little ball," she'd say, whistling softly as if calling a dog. "C'mere, little guy. I promise I'll treat you better next time."

She caught me on the sixteenth green, almost a month

before my twenty-eighth birthday. I was hiding in a stand of trees, watching her putt, wet to the knees from a detour through a water hazard. It was an easy shot, eight inches at the outside, but she missed it anyway, the ball rimming out of the cup and settling a foot from the hole. Delia swore prettily and tapped the putter against the bottom of her shoe. She said, "Why don't you come on out? I can't concentrate with you back there."

She wiped her brow and looked in my direction. I hunched down, tried to make myself smaller. I didn't quite believe that she was talking to me. I could hear a sprinkler going in the distance, could feel the hairs on the back of my neck. My heart was like a ricochet. Delia brandished the putter above her head with both hands and said, "All right. If you won't come out, I'm coming in after you."

Then she came stalking across the green in big, determined steps, her knees flashing at the hem of her shorts. I considered making a break, but I couldn't figure a way out of the rough without her identifying me anyway, so I stepped sheepishly from behind the trees and held my hands up in surrender.

"It's me," I said. "It's Simon Bell."

"Simon?" She lowered the putter and looked at me. "How long have you been following me? I heard you crashing around back on eleven."

"A few weeks," I said.

"A few weeks?" she said, arching her eyebrows. "I meant how long today."

She tilted her head slightly and squinted at me as if examining a blurred photograph. There was one of those early moons pressing against the sky, and all around us I could hear crickets in the grass, night making an entrance. "A few weeks," she said again, her voice going gentle and amused, like that was the sweetest thing she had heard in a long time.

More Than One Way to Steal a Heart

Delia Holladay was a housekeeper's daughter. She was still too young for school then, and her mother would bring her along most days, leave her on the living room couch in a stranger's house, the black and white television muttering quietly, or set her to work on simpler tasks, emptying wastebaskets, wiping countertops, working a feather duster around alarm clocks and little dishes full of change and framed photographs of people she didn't know.

Sometimes Delia, this little girl with skinny legs and ragged knees, with a rib cage like a dish drain and arms as lean and hard as a boy's, would be left alone in a well-appointed bedroom, heavy curtains fanning beside the windows, silk pillows piled against the headboard of the bed, and sometimes she would find herself, almost against her will, standing in a walk-in closet, rows of dresses hanging around her like tired ghosts. She knew she would be skinned alive—her mother's favorite threat—if she were discovered, but the desire was so strong, she couldn't help herself. While her mother ironed or washed the dishes by hand, making other people's messes disappear, Delia would press her cheeks against crisp evening gowns and slip negligees over her tank tops and cut-off jeans. She'd pose in front of a mirror in someone else's lingerie and apply a little color to her lips, just for one look at herself, a glimpse into the future, a few seconds as a woman. Delia with her hair cropped short like a boy and her reckless elbows.

And sometimes, while her mother ran the vacuum cleaner, Delia would rifle through drawers in a polished bureau and choose one thing, just one, maybe a scarf that looked as though it hadn't been worn in a while or a tarnished money clip or an earring without a mate or a pair of pantyhose or a discarded leather watchband, nothing of real value, and slip it into her pocket and make it her own. She kept her takings in a Red Goose shoe box under her bed. At night, when the house was quiet except for the synchronized snoring of her brothers, she'd open the lid and have a look at her takings, other people's smells lifting up to her from the box, expensive perfume and animal skins and cool metals and what she believed must surely be a sort of joy.

Her father taught her to play the piano when she was eight years old. He worked at the Ramada Inn, doing standards for tourists, splitting the money that collected in his jar with the bartender. She had his careful hands and his ear for pitch and, to a degree, his love for music. Her parents couldn't afford a piano so her father took an old card table and a black marking pen and drew diagrams of the keyboard on opposite sides. He would sit across from her and tell her to imitate the position of his fingers on the imaginary keys, first the major and minor chords, then scales, then simple songs that she could play with one hand. Her father hummed along while she tapped out notes, unsure of her accuracy because she couldn't hear the music, her fingertips making a steady wincing sound, her father hunched close to watch her hands, nodding his head as if he could hear real music tumbling out of the table.

Nights she'd go with her mother down to the Ramada and watch her father play for as long as she could keep her eyes open, then fall asleep curled head to foot with her mother around one of the big horseshoe-shaped booths at the back of the bar. When he was finished, he would shake her shoulder gently and lead her over to the piano and let her have an hour or so while the staff cleaned around her. Delia loved those hours—Felix the Bartender shushing around with a push broom and the waitresses gathered at a table by the piano smoking cigarettes and counting tips. Even when she hit a sour chord, she loved the sound the piano made, full and rich and resonant as night.

When her father wasn't playing the piano, he was home, working on an old MG convertible in the backyard. That always made perfect sense to her, engine work and piano playing, delicate tasks done with the hands. She would sit in the driver's seat while her father tinkered and listen to him talk about howling down the highway with the top down, on up into Canada or Alaska maybe. The hood blocked her view of him and his voice, muffled and disembodied, sounded eerie to Delia. She didn't notice then that when her father talked about driving to Alaska he always said "I" and never "we" or "us."

Her father liked how on warm nights the labels of beer bottles would slip off sticky in your hands. He did not like the way he met his wife, which was through the classified ads. He was embarrassed that he couldn't find a woman on his own. He always said he placed the ad on a bet, but Delia suspected he was lying. His ad read SMALL WHITE MAN, 5'4, SEEKS WHITE WOMAN WITH BIG HEART and he liked that. Her father thought that was very clever and so did her mother. They lived near the paper mill, and his idea of a perfect evening was driving up to the top of the red clay bluffs north of town and trying to pick out their house among all the distant, flickering lights in windows. They could always agree on which house was theirs, though Delia doubted that they were ever right.

When he left for good, Delia was fourteen. The first thing her mother did was buy Delia a piano, used and battered and expensive, and it hunched in the corner of the den, taking up too much space. She said, "At least he left you what was good in him. You shouldn't lose that."

She was teaching by the time she met Sam Holladay. She had taken a job at the public school in Sherwood, directing the chorus and organizing recitals for her students. Sam Holladay saw her in the wings of the stage. This young woman gesturing frantically at the performers, moving her lips, strangely, as if urging the proper notes from the piano with her voice. She was slender and a little awkward, with green eyes. She had an unpretending elegance about her. The old auditorium was without air-conditioning and the crowd was wasting away in the close air, but she seemed strangely unaffected, her face dry, her motion easy, as if she had discovered a remedy for summer in Alabama that no one else had ever heard of. He approached her after the show, found her backstage shepherding the children. His opening line, which he'd been considering all evening, was, "My name is Sam Holladay. I know all the history of the world."

Six weeks later, they were married. Delia believed herself to be in love with this man, who taught history and who moved in that pleasingly precarious way that tall people have, like their bones can't quite hold them the way they used to. He had a sweep of moon-white hair and a soft stomach and heavy arms. When he held her, really gathered her to him for the first time, they were leaning against a Cadillac in the parking lot of her apartment complex waiting for a locksmith to arrive. It was the night of their first official date, and Sam had locked his keys in his car with the engine running, and she found his absent-mindedness attractive. For two hours, they waited. The city was full of troublesome locks. She made the occasional trip upstairs for more beer and they talked—he about history, the immense scope of the world and the way everything ran in cycles, she about a house full of brothers in Mississippi—told each other the things that everyone tells as a way of revealing something about themselves. Cats nosed around the Dumpster, mewing softly. Every now and then, a car pulled into the lot and they stopped talking and squinted into the headlights, trying to see if the locksmith had arrived. If Delia knew the driver, she'd wave and Sam would raise his beer in greeting. A short silence would fall, but it wasn't an uncomfortable sort of quiet—the two of them gathering their thoughts, the air damp from the afternoon rain. After a while, she said, "Are you ever going to kiss me, Sam?"

He leaned in too fast, their teeth bumping hard. He didn't know what to do with his hands, but when he managed, finally, to get them situated around her back and shoulders, she felt like he was covering her completely, the night air touching not a single molecule of her skin.

This was the man she married, all flesh and warmth and forgetfulness. He was gentle as a Saint Bernard with his students. She moved into his house on the golf course, not unlike the houses she had helped her mother clean as a little girl. They drove to school together in the mornings, home together at night, and she began to see a picture of her life stretching out before her like a sheet of music, the borders clear, the tone defined. It was not an entirely unpleasant idea, this life, just not quite the one she'd imagined for herself.

One night, lying in bed, she decided to tell Sam a story.

"There was a creek behind my family's house," she said. "A little stream, really, but in the winter it would swell and run fast enough to be dangerous. Dangerous to a child, anyway. I remember when I was ten there was this crazy ice storm. No one knew what to do in an ice storm. We'd never seen anything like it. And this was serious. Snapping whole trees. Power outages. Everything."

She paused, propped up on her elbow. She took a breath. The curtains billowed lightly in the breeze. He didn't make a sound.

She said, "My brothers stole some beer from the fridge and took a flashlight and I followed them down to the water. We could hear it from the house and we wanted to see it. There were these pieces of ice whipping around. It sounded like the river was full of broken glass. And there was this beaver dam that had a section ripped out of it by the current, that was all jagged and frozen over."

She could see the silhouette of his shoulder in the darkness and she shook him. "You awake?" she said.

He grunted and said he was, rolled on his side to face her.

"We watched this tree," she said, "an entire uprooted tree, roots and all, get pulled through. It was the worst sound I ever heard and it came out in splinters. Completely mangled. I remember watching that tree go through and come out torn, and watching the light bouncing off the ice and the whitewater and wanting to jump in. Can you believe it? Jump right in after I had seen what had happened to the tree. It wasn't that I wanted to kill myself or anything. I think I wanted to see if I could outswim the current or come through that gap somehow undamaged. I know it's crazy. My mother was worried sick when we got back. She had reason to be. I don't know what made me think of that just now. You still awake?"

He didn't answer. She shook him again, and he snorted, flopped over on his back, his chest lifting and sagging heavily with sleep. "You're always saying you want to know things about me," she whispered. "There you go. That's something." She was awake for a long time after that, her muscles shaking like a faint current of electricity was passing through her.

She felt a similar sort of energy the day Simon Bell told her where his father died. There was an electric warmth along the bottoms of her feet and the hair on her arms and neck stood on end like the air was full of static. Evening light danced across the surface of the pool. He had been looking at her in that tired and familiar way that men have, as though trying to commit her shape to memory. But now, she recognized a sadness in him that she hadn't seen before, though she suspected it had been there all along. She took a step toward him, and stopped, let her fingers linger for a moment on the top of his head, as if to offer comfort, then hurried home and didn't go back for three days.

None of this did she mention to her husband. She went on with the ordinary pace of her days, finishing up the last of her paperwork at school before summer vacation, cooking dinner with Sam and eating at the wooden table in the kitchen, then settling in front of the television to watch a movie on the VCR.

At night, she let her husband tell her stories to put her to sleep, sometimes from history and myth—Ovid watching his nameless love at a Roman cocktail party, Menelaus courting war to reclaim his wife—and sometimes the story of their future together, simple inventions, full of country houses and rocking chairs and dogs in open fields. Every now and then, she would lose track of what she was doing and find herself remembering her mother polishing someone else's silver or her father peeking around the hood of his MG to give her a smile, and somehow she was also recalling Simon Bell. The image of his face hovered just beyond the reach of her memory. She had to remind herself that nothing unusual had happened, that there were no secrets to keep.

When she discovered that she was being followed on the golf course, she felt the current a third time, first from fear, then, as she listened to him crashing around in the brush—she assumed it was a man—from amusement and simple wonder. She wasn't worried exactly; she believed that she could handle herself. Intrigued was closer to the truth, or thrilled or aroused or anxious, some combination of emotions that produced a definite tingling at the base of her spine. To her surprise, it was Simon Bell, looking so pathetic when he emerged from the pines, soaked to the knees, his hair a mess of tangles and sweat, his forearms and face tracked with scratches.

She took him home and fixed them each a beer in the kitchen and loaned him a pair of her husband's shorts while his pants were in the dryer. Here was this man who had been spying on her for weeks, he'd said, and strangely, she found the idea romantic in a sad way; Simon Bell pining along in her wake, the way she found it endearing when one of her students developed a crush on her. He had washed his arms and his face, the hair at his part still damp. She was sitting on the counter, letting one leg swing out and thump back against the cabinet. Simon was standing by the sink. While he was talking—telling a story about a wave of burglaries in the neighborhood when he was a boy—she closed her eyes. She lifted her chin to the sun through the windows. Blind, she could hear everything, distant voices, like the intercepted bursts of a radio transmission, hungry birds, faint music from somewhere, her awkward heart, the whole day washed in sibilant noise.

"Let's get drunk," she said.

"You want to get drunk?"

"Isn't that what they do in the movies?" she said. "Whenever people are about to make a mistake, they get drunk."

"I don't watch many movies," he said. He walked over and stood between her knees and she could feel the places where their bodies met, his hipbones against the insides of her thighs, her wrists resting on his shoulders, his forearms at her waist, where he was bracing himself against the counter. He said, "I can't think of anything to say that hasn't been said before."

"All the good lines are used up," she said. "I keep wanting to remind you that I'm a married woman. I'm not sure who's seducing who here."

"You're seducing me," he said.

"All right," she said.

When she kissed him, she could smell cut grass. No more of her husband's aftershave or the warm smell of the dryer, just the grass. It smelled gigantic and she wondered if there wasn't a little sunheat or something in there, too, giving it a simmer. She was light and alive. It seemed to her, at that moment, that this kiss and whatever happened next was a thing apart from her marriage, wholly separate. She could do this and still love her husband. She pulled away, just for a second, and she would have sworn she could see the sunlight on Simon's teeth and in his eyes. He reached up and held her face with both hands. They kissed the rough kiss of drunks, both of them thinking they knew exactly what was happening, exactly how all of this, all the hands on backs and closed eyes and surging blood, was going to end.

Buying a Gun
in New Orleans

Sam Holladay bought the gun on his honeymoon. He and Delia had driven down to New Orleans to be married, and as they were emerging from the courthouse, the sunlight as bright as he'd ever seen it, a white man in a white linen suit walked up and asked him for the time. Later, he would remember how beautiful Delia looked in her brown dress with white polka dots, the way her heels pressed her pelvis forward and made her calves go all ropy and lean, the way her hair played against her back. He would remember how glad he was to stop and give this man the time, how proud he was of his young bride, how he wanted everyone to know that she belonged to him. And he would recall a woman standing on a wrought-iron balcony of the building across the street, watching the three of them, this stranger in a white linen suit and Sam Holladay and his wife, and how in the space of time it took for him to look at his watch, the woman on the balcony had disappeared and the stranger produced a slender ice pick from nowhere, like a trick of prestidigitation.

Sam lost his wallet and the very watch that had distracted

him, and Delia gave up a strand of pearls, but on the way back to their hotel, she said, "Don't worry, Sam. Those pearls were as fake as a movie sunset."

Both of them lost their wedding rings. Sam Holladay lost a large measure of his pride, and they lost the time spent at the police station, when they should have been between the clean sheets in their room, celebrating the day. That was the part that surprised him most. How excited Delia was by the whole thing, how she made love recklessly and violently and without restraint, straddling him, the tendons in her neck drawn tight, and then she'd asked him to move around behind her, her back arched, his fingers in her mouth, her eyes on their reflection in the bureau mirror. When they were finished, she said, "Can you believe it? He took us right in front of the courthouse. The goddam courthouse."

She had her head on his shoulder, the music and voices of Bourbon Street drifting up to them, faintly, as if from miles away. Her hair smelled like flowers.

"You can never find a cop when you need one," he said. "That old saw."

The next morning, while Delia was still asleep, Sam Holladay crept out of bed, went down to the street, and found a pawn shop on Tchopatulous. There was the five-day waiting period to deal with, but the owner thought Sam looked respectable enough and went ahead and sold him the .38, banking that his record would come up clear, and it did. For the rest of the trip, Sam carried the gun tucked in his pants at the small of his back, hidden beneath the hem of his sportcoat. He paraded his wife up and down Bourbon Street with confidence, cut through back alleys pungent with decay, secure in the knowledge that now, if called upon to do so, he could protect her.

For a year, the gun stayed in a hatbox on a shelf in the silver closet beneath an old fedora that had belonged to his father. On holidays, Delia took down the good flatware and the linen tablecloth, never even knowing it existed. The shelf was high enough that she had to ask Sam for help if she needed something.

In April of their first year together, she shook him awake one night and said that she'd heard footsteps. Someone was in the house. The air conditioner was broken at the time and the bedroom was too warm. He could feel a faint film of sweat on her palms. He was bleary and thick-headed with sleep, but he touched a finger to his lips and got out of bed and made his way down the hall as quietly as he could. Sam Holladay stood in the dark hallway and listened for a long time. Nothing. The house creaked and settled its weight. He wondered if he could get to the silver closet without being seen by an intruder. He took a few steps. Still nothing. After a while, Delia's voice from the bedroom, "Sam, you all right? I don't hear anything anymore. You're scaring me, Sam. Are you okay?"

"I'm fine," he said, feeling such an overwhelming tenderness for this woman he could hardly breathe. "Nobody's here. Situation normal."

He crept to the silver closet, took down the gun, and slipped it under the mattress, just as Delia was kneeling on the bed to embrace him, and there it stayed, untouched, until the day he used it to kill Simon Bell.

Divining for Gold

Betty Fowler saw it happen. She was on the sixteenth fairway of the Speaking Pines golf course when the Holladays' old Cadillac came swinging into the driveway on their way back from church. Simon Bell must have seen it, too. He crossed the lawn to the car, pressing his hands flat against the passenger window. She watched Sam Holladay get out, watched Delia slip past on his side. When Simon rushed around behind the car as if to catch her, Sam met him in the driveway, held his arms while Delia ducked into the house. He walked Simon back into his own yard. They stood there talking for a minute, almost casually, the way neighbors might have a conversation if they happened to meet on the grass. The lawn was neatly cut. Sam went inside and Simon waited, sitting Indian-style in the yard, his eyes sweeping over the golf course, but blankly, like he wasn't really seeing. After a while, Sam reappeared, moving with determination, something in his hand.

She wasn't playing golf when it happened. Betty Fowler

was divining for gold. You could find her almost any evening, when the weather was nice, out on the golf course between six o'clock and darkness, a forked hazel branch in her hands. Twenty-five years ago, her husband had owned all of the property for miles around—the golf course, the lots on which the pretty houses stood. The road, now blacktop, had been covered in cockle shells, white and dry as bone, before his business failed and he'd had to sell off the land a little at a time, first to the country club, then to the developer who had subdivided within eight months. During leaner years, her husband would tell a story about how, when he sensed the beginning of the end, he had buried a chest of gold coins—bought at auction before they were married—somewhere out there among the pristine fairways, the immaculate greens. It made him feel better to believe that a fortune was buried beneath his feet.

Betty Fowler told all of this to Sheriff Nightingale when he came by to ask her what she knew. She told him how she'd read books on divining—you could find them right in the public library, she said—told him how she had never known her husband to speak a word that wasn't true. Why should she stop believing him now that he was dead? The sheriff listened patiently, drank her iced tea. What she didn't tell him was how she knew to look. She had been standing in the fairway with her eyes closed, holding the forked ends of the rod with both hands, just like the books said. She'd been at it for years and never heard a word from her divining rod. But that day, there in the damp July heat, she felt it twitch, felt a tremor in her hands, like a dream of electricity. She turned the way it seemed that the rod wanted her to turn and opened her eyes and there was the Cadillac. And then Simon. And then Sam Holladay bringing his hand up, gently, like he was going to touch Simon's heart.

She told him that the sound was like dropping a stone into water. It was hardly a sound at all. He said, "Probably the shot was muffled by his chest. You know how in movies they always cover the gun with a pillow. Same thing."

Betty Fowler lived a few houses down from the bend in the road where the golf course made the slow turn back toward the clubhouse. She looked at the sheriff, perspiring in his uniform. His shadow on the windows made it possible to see inside the house, the china cabinet, her porcelain figurines, white doilies on the end tables, all the trappings of the antique. She didn't want him to leave. She turned her mind over for a detail she might have missed, the stubble on Simon's cheeks, the way he fell, feet and head going parallel in the air like a magic act volunteer. But she'd already told him everything she could.

When he asked, "What about before? You didn't see anything unusual?"

She said, "You know what I've been learning to do in my old age? I've been learning how to cuss. Listen." She arranged her mouth like someone speaking an unfamiliar language, clipping her lower lip with her top teeth. She said, "Fuuuck," drawing the word out in a country way.

"I need to get going," he said.

"You try it," she said. "Fuuuck."

"I don't think so," he said.

"C'mon," she said. "It's fun."

She followed him out to the driveway, still muttering profanities under her breath. When they reached his car, she fished in one of the gardening pockets on her dress and came out with a silver dollar, like she'd planned this moment all along. The sheriff waited patiently. She held the coin between her thumb and index finger. Her other hand she whipped through his line of sight, so quick he almost didn't notice the gesture, and after it had passed, the silver dollar was gone. Both hands she presented to him, palms down, thumbs tucked under.

"I know this trick," he said. "You hide it in one hand and tell me it's behind my ear or something, right? My daddy used to do it."

"You'd be surprised." She turned her hands over, revealing pale, empty palms. "They were in love," she said. "I think they were."

"Who was, Mrs. Fowler?" he said. "Who was in love?"

Without saying anything else, without ever producing the coin, she patted his arm, like they were old friends and she was sorry to see him go, and smiled and walked away. When she reached the four steps up to the porch, she paused, hitched her gait, gripped the rail with her right hand. She climbed the stairs gingerly, like an old woman, and he liked her better for it. It made him feel like he knew something about her.

Part 2

It's awfully easy to be hardboiled about everything in the daytime, but at night it is another thing.

—Ernest Hemingway

A History Lesson

At twenty, Sam Holladay decided never to fall in love. This was in the fall of 1952, and he had been seeing a woman named Mary Youngblood who was also a student at the University of Alabama. She was tall with reddish-brown hair, hair the color of pine straw, and she had inspired him to stand in front of the mirror and practice speaking words that he had never said before: I love you like the sky, he would mouth to his own face in the glass, crewcut and lean and big-eared, I love you more than life itself, the phrases lifted from romantic novels. It surprised him how easy it was to imagine being in love with Mary Youngblood. As simply as if it were the truth, he could daydream the two of them pushing a shopping cart, taking turns making selections from the shelves, or lying side by side in a bed he'd never seen before, each confident of the other's presence even in their sleep.

When he finally spoke the words aloud, he and Mary were sitting on the steps of the women's dormitory, each wearing one of her white mittens because he'd forgotten to bring his gloves. He was always forgetting things. She bumped her shoulder against his, then said she needed to be getting to bed. It was almost curfew time. She stood and kissed the top of his head and slipped through the doors, leaving him dazed and breathless and feeling as though a husk of rough fabric had been placed between the world and his heart. He didn't say the words again until he met Delia Simpson.

When he first saw her, standing in the wings of the stage, he went deaf for a moment, stopped hearing the awkward clamor of childish fingers on piano keys and tried to imagine something to say to such a young and beautiful woman. What were young men telling pretty girls these days? Then, without willing it, he saw the two of them washing dishes together, laughing familiarly about his frightened deliberations over an opening line. It would become a part of their shared history, a story to tell as a reminder of what had passed between them. When sound came back to him, the auditorium was full of applause.

She took him to meet her mother in June, three days after he had asked her to marry him. The age difference made him anxious and doubtful, and he found himself again, forty-years later, practicing at the mirror, this time in his house on Speaking Pines Road: Hello, Mrs. Simpson. It's a pleasure to meet you, Mrs. Simpson. I love your daughter, Mrs. Simpson. The bathroom was a testament to his age and bachelorhood: white whiskers in the basin from his morning shave, calcium tablets in the medicine cabinet for his tiring bones. He felt ridiculous and terrified and as sure of his heart as he had ever been.

When Delia's mother greeted them at the door, he said, "Hello, Mrs.— It's nice to finally— I've heard a lot about you, Mrs. Simpson."

"Oh, Lord," she said, cutting her eyes to Delia as if they were sharing a private joke. "You can drop the missus. You're too old even to be dating me."

"Mom," Delia said, "be nice. Sam's the man I'm going to marry."

"Is that right, Mr. Holladay?" she said. "Are you going to marry my daughter who's too young for you by about thirty years?"

"Yes," he said, the words catching in his throat. "I love her very much."

Right at that moment, he thought of Mary Youngblood. Standing in the open doorway of Delia's mother's house, crickets ringing in the yard behind him like sleigh bells, he remembered the way her lips had felt against his hair and that she had forgotten her mitten and been too embarrassed to retrieve it because she had ended things between them the next day. He remembered, as well, the decision he had made—the sort of decision that only a young man can make, sure of the future and foolish with conceit—never to love another woman as long as he lived. He smiled at Delia's mother and felt a sudden, sad surprise that he had kept his promise to himself for so long. He hadn't done it deliberately. He'd forgotten it, in fact, with other women, at other times. But here he was sixty-two years old, unaccompanied and unloved for the better part of his days.

Later, when Delia had gone to wash her hands, Mrs. Simpson said, "I don't mean this in a cruel way, Sam, but one thing I'm glad about tonight is that you're too old to leave my daughter."

She crossed her legs and looked at him, as though waiting for a reaction. He didn't say anything for a while. He wanted to tell her that he would make another promise, not just the marriage vows but something more permanent and real. He loved her daughter—he knew that—and he would do anything in his power to keep them from ever being apart.

Rabbit's Feet, Religion, and Other Superstitions

From my father, I inherited a house, a car, blue eyes, one arm that is slightly but not noticeably longer than the other, and an innate impatience for superstitious people. They tend to be overindulgent worriers, he told me, never responsible for their own mistakes. When he wanted to give me some advice, he would take me to the golf course across the street from our house, and we would walk along the soft grass of the sixteenth fairway, the last of the daylight catching in the treetops. My father would still be wearing his suit and tie, but he would carry his shoes in one hand, his bare feet as white as new golf balls, and a drink in the other, the ice ticking against the sides of his glass like sailboat rigging. We'd have the whole, discreet course to ourselves.

"You can't trust a wood-knocker, Simon." He lumped all forms of nonscientific belief into one lamentable, amorphous school of thought. "Or a Bible thumper. Or a reader of horoscopes."

He did a broad expansive gesture, indicating the stars. My father had a funny, stilted way of speaking when he was telling me something he thought was important. He wasn't a big man, but he moved like one. There was something in his bearing, his tendency to exaggerate. He occupied a considerable amount of space for a man of average size. He said, "If they had their way, we'd still be reading sheep guts to tell the future. Hell," he said, "we'd still be sacrificing virgins."

"What's a virgin?" I said. I was seven years old.

Years later, the thing that would stand out about the way my father managed his advice and explanation—covering everything from sexual procedure to the historical significance of the virgin—was that he was able to deliver it without demeaning my mother in any way. Despite the fact that she went to church every Sunday and owned a rabbit's foot key chain and lifted her feet whenever our car rattled across a set of railroad tracks, he somehow made it sound like she alone, out of all the superstitious people on earth, was worthy of love, regardless of what he told me about the world.

I often wondered what it was that kept them together, what kept them whirling around each other like wild planets. When they argued, my mother would come to my room and sit on the foot of my bed and talk to me while she brushed her hair. We didn't talk about anything important, just school or my friends or a movie I'd seen. She sat facing my desk and pulled the brush through her long hair, static bristling, until it was smooth and fine.

Every Fourth of July, my mother had a party. They were mostly her friends, tellers from the bank where she used to work and couples from the neighborhood. My father wasn't much for socializing. Everyone drank fruity cocktails, and my mother flitted through the crowd, pirouetting now and then to speak to one of her guests. After a few drinks, she went barefoot and no one cared. My father would spend an hour, maybe a little less, being nice, then he'd slip away and sit on the stairs and watch my mother. Her smile flickering, her fingers dancing on her hands. My room was at the top of the stairs, and I would hide in my doorway and spy on both of them, watch him watching her. After dark, the entire crew from my mother's party would cross the street and spread blankets on the golf course to watch the country club fireworks. There was always someone who'd had too much to drink, who staggered around and made lewd jokes, who flirted with women who weren't his wife. I remember once this guy with a soft paunch and broad shoulders and a kind face kept throwing his arm around my mother and whispering in her ear. My father told me to stay where I was—we were sitting together in the grass; I was always in his shadow then—and walked over to the man and my mother, stepping across the summery legs of lounging guests. Without a word, he punched the man in the stomach with his left hand. That was the last of my mother's parties. The fireworks started up as my father was walking back to the house, bright sparks like falling stars.

Not two weeks later, my father rented a house on the Gulf of Mexico for the rest of the summer. Close to where my mother died. The house was two-story, raised on sandstone pillars to let the water pass beneath it during storm tides. He made the two-hour commute to and from the city every day. He didn't leave us a second car, so Mother and I dawdled on the beach, building elaborate sand castles, looking for shells. She swam an hour every morning. She was a strong swimmer and that summer her shoulders broadened, her arms got hard and lean.

My father brought her horror movies from town. We grilled hot dogs and hamburgers and my father bought a device for making your own ice cream. Everyone was trying very hard to have a good time. On weekends, my father stood in the shorebreak and cast fishing line out over the sandbar. My mother and I sat on the sand and watched him, cheered him on, but he never caught anything. His shoulders burned in the sun, skin flaking away like parchment.

The walls of the house were thin and sound traveled through them as easily as over water. I could hear my father getting himself ready in the morning, running water to shave, thumping around in the kitchen. He'd wake me up and fix me a bowl of cereal or scramble an egg, and the two of us would sit in the kitchen as my mother got herself together. We listened to her singing in the shower. At night, I could hear them in the bedroom, their voices and other sounds. I couldn't sleep one night and wandered into their room, and there was a great heaving beneath the sheets. My father sat up, panting, and said, "What're you doing, boy? How 'bout a little privacy here." His voice sounded angry, but I didn't think he was angry with me. He looked old in the moonlight.

I could hear them arguing other nights. I couldn't make out everything, but I once heard my mother say, "I feel like a prisoner." And my father said, "You did what you did."

A few minutes later he appeared at my door, his shape a silhouette against the light from the hall. "You awake," he said. He got me out of bed and into a pair of swim trunks. "Night diving," he said. "Get us out of the house. It'll be an adventure." We carried his scuba diving equipment down to the beach, floated the tank out past the sand bar on the buoyancy vest. He strapped me into a weight belt, and I rode his back out to the deeper water. When he was satisfied with the depth, he pushed the regulator against my lips and told me to breathe. He began letting air out of the BCD and we sank like a pair of stones. The Gulf was so dark and heavy with all the summer rain that we could barely see each other, couldn't really, just a sense of not being alone, but I froze the first time he took the mouthpiece from me to get a breath for himself. The water was soundless but for the bubbles, and I forgot myself in panic, in the sound of the bubbles and my heartbeat, forgot even where I was or why I was so afraid, there, ten feet underwater with my feet pressed firmly to the sea floor with the gravity of my father's weight belt. Until he forced the mouthpiece between my teeth and the bone dry air into me.

Later, safely in my room, my mother sat beside me on the bed and touched my forehead. I could hear the ocean, could still feel it in my arms and legs.

"Your hair's wet," she said.

"I know," I said. "I'll catch cold."

"That's right," she said.

When she didn't say anything else, I lay back and closed my eyes. After a few minutes, I felt her shifting on the mattress, stretching out beside me, our shoulders touching, the way she did when I'd stayed up watching one of her horror movies and couldn't sleep for dreaming.

I told Delia all of this during our first week together, told her how I couldn't be sure that my mother had had an affair, that my father was often quick to suspect other people's motives and even swifter and more definite in his response. I told her about his union busting—though he was right about that—and about the time he discovered fifty dollars missing from his wallet and accused me of stealing it. He was mistaken and he had no proof, but he made me do hard labor around the yard anyway, working me from the end of school until darkness every day for a week. The money turned up a few days later in his dry cleaning and he gave it to me, said he was sorry, told me that I was a hard worker and deserved an honest week's wage. Fifty dollars seemed a little short for that much work, but I didn't complain. An apology from my father was a rare thing indeed. He almost never second-guessed himself, even when the thing he might have put at risk with a false accusation was his marriage. Plus, I didn't believe for a minute that my mother had it in her to love another man.

During the summer, Sam Holladay taught an evening class at the community college so the hours between five-thirty and nine o'clock belonged to Delia and me. I gave her a spare key and sometimes she'd be waiting when I came home from work, arranged in my bed with a movie on HBO, one hand holding the sheet over her bare chest. She liked to watch me undress, said she wanted me to pretend that I was alone and go about my business the way I would have if I wasn't sleeping with my next-door neighbor's wife. I kept my back to her, took off my tie and draped it on the rack, found a wooden hanger for my suit, desire building in me all the while.

"Why couldn't your mother have been in love with another man?" she said.

"I don't know," I said over my shoulder. "Because she was my mother."

"That's no reason," she said.

I worked the buttons on my shirt, my eyes on the neat row of shoes in the closet. I heard Delia gliding out of bed behind me and padding across the carpet. She ran her hands over my hips and linked her fingers on my stomach. Her breasts were warm against my back. I said, "Are you all the way undressed?"

"I still have on underwear," she said. "Do you want me to take it off?"

"Yes," I said.

"Don't turn around," she said. I heard her rustling, the whisper of fabric on skin, then the tiny thump of her heel hitting the ground. "You can't look until you tell me something else about your mother."

Delia was always asking about my mother. I didn't mind talking about her much. When I told the stories to Delia, they began to seem less like something that might have happened in my own life and more like the sort of thing you would see in a movie. We traded stories—my childhood for hers—and made love, daylight going scarce beyond the windows, the two of us winding together in the guest room of my parents' house. I had tried sleeping in my old room when I first moved back into the house, but the bunkbeds felt childish and confining and the walls were covered in Alabama football pennants and posters of rock bands that embarrassed me now. And I couldn't sleep in my parents' room. It still smelled like them, his cigarettes and her perfume and that other more familiar smell that people leave on their pillows and clothes. The guest room was decorated in that neutrally tasteful way that all good guest rooms have, designed to make just about anyone feel at home, beige curtains and matching comforter on the double bed, maroon dust ruffle, framed Audubon prints on the walls. The window looked out over the pool and I could see it, when I forgot to turn the underwater lights off, glowing in the darkness like a giant radioactive lozenge.

Some days, Delia would ask me to drive her around Sherwood so we could keep an eye out for the alleged other man. She'd point at men on the sidewalk or in passing cars and say, "Could that be him? Could that be him?" But when I tried to imagine the man for Delia, he began to resemble an aging film star whose name I couldn't recall, gone to fat by the time I was born and put out to pasture in television and low-budget films. "Don't you want to know who he is?" Delia said. "He's the only person who knows what really happened."

"It doesn't matter," I said. "Let's go home and get in bed."

It was raining hard outside and we were parked across from The First Bank of Sherwood, because Delia had the idea that my mother must have met the man while she was still a teller. The bank was closed but there were a few lights in the offices upstairs. Every now and then a man would come through the revolving doors huddled in a raincoat or hunched beneath an umbrella, but we were too far away to make out physical detail. Delia hung her head out the window and eyed them through the rain. When she pulled herself back inside, her cheeks were running with water. She pushed her hair back, flattening the rain out with her palms, and licked rainwater from her lips.

"I can't see a thing," she said. "Can't we get closer?"

"He'll see us if we try to cross the street," I said. "Besides, the man my father punched was taller than that guy. He'd be a few years older, too, I think."

I propped my head in one hand and traced my fingers

along the line of her neck, over her cheeks, down her nose, the way a blind person figures out what someone looks like. My insides were going crazy, but I forced myself to be gentle. She closed her eyes. When I touched her lips, she smiled and said, "You're just humoring me aren't you? You're making all this up as you go along."

"Maybe a little," I said.

"Asshole," she said. She leaned over and kissed the side of my face, the tip of her nose cold from the air conditioner and the rain. "This could be important."

Later, I kept thinking of the word *adultery*, running it through my mind in search of euphemisms and synonyms but I couldn't think of another word that matched what we were doing, lying side by side in bed now, naked and pleasantly exhausted and adrenalized by a surprise visit from Louise Caldwell, who was collecting for the neighborhood watch. Criminals don't wait for good weather, she had said, when I wrapped myself in a robe and met her at the door. She was wearing a clear plastic rain hat, though the shower had tapered off by then. We had both agreed that vigilance was a good thing, rain or shine. Delia shifted on the mattress, said it was almost time for her to be getting home, and I wanted it to be possible for the two of us to have been drawn together by a set of emotions altogether different from the usual bitterness and despair. A longing gorgeous enough to be worthy of the sin, an excess of capacity in the heart.

The day was closing palpably beyond the windows. I sat up and moved to the end of the bed and pulled on my pants. Delia linked her hands behind her head, lifting her breasts, flattening her stomach. She said, "Have you ever seen that optometrist's commercial where the fat woman is trying on new glasses and when she looks in the mirror she's skinny and beautiful all of a sudden? When she goes outside her shitty old car is a Porsche and her kids are quiet and well behaved and don't have chocolate all over their faces anymore?"

"I told you I don't watch television," I said.

"Maybe that's how it was for your mother," she said. "Not that your father was bad, but that this other guy made the world look different, see what I mean? Not better or worse, just different. That's something I could understand."

"This conversation is making my stomach hurt," I said. "Can we talk about something else? Let's talk about you for a while."

She sighed and pressed her toes against the small of my back. "I once killed a man just for snoring too loud," she said, doing some kind of twangy gunslinger voice. "I once killed a man just to watch him die."

"That's John Wesley Hardin from the Time Life Books commercial," I said.

"I thought you didn't watch television," she said.

She sat up behind me and draped her arms around my shoulders and pinched my earlobe between her teeth. I said that I had to watch TV sometimes to know for certain whether I liked it or not and she told me happily that she would never believe another word I said.

When Delia was gone and night had settled in, I walked out on my front steps and found my neighbor Bob Robinson outside rooting through his trash can. The houses were dark and pretty, their residents asleep. The golf course as neat and quiet as the moon. I could see the blue light of a television in a dark room, streamers of toilet paper in the Caldwells' trees.

"Hungry, Bob?" I said.

He started, then got himself together and scratched his bare belly.

"Misplaced something," he said, stifling a yawn. "Thought the wife might have thrown it out by mistake."

Bob was closing in on fifty, had a horseshoe fringe of hair around his skull like a monk. I liked Bob because he moved to the neighborhood after my parents had died. He didn't know anything about me, except that I was his neighbor, an attorney, respectable by all appearances.

When his family first moved to town, he came to my door and said that they didn't know anyone around here, but he had to list three local emergency names and numbers for his children's school. He wanted to know if I would mind if he listed me. His wife had sent along a devil's food cake, and he said they'd thought I looked like a nice-enough guy. I told him nothing would make me happier. I invited him in for a beer and we talked about football, about hunting and fishing. We toed the floor with our shoes. After a while, his children, two boys and a girl, showed up with news that dinner was ready. The children rushed past me and clutched their father, pulling him to the door. Duty calls, he said, and that seemed like the most perfect exit line in the world.

"What about you?" he said. "You wouldn't be interested in a drink this time of night would you? I'm buying." He pulled a pint of bourbon from the big pocket on his robe, shook it beside his ear like he was trying to determine the contents of a Christmas package.

Bob was from Indiana or Iowa or someplace, came to Alabama to take a vice president's job at the paper plant. The two of us sat on the curb in the warm darkness and passed the bottle back and forth. A car made the curve in front of the house, a little too slow for this time of night, and both of us eyed it past, making sure the driver understood that one or two of us were still awake, still wary. I said, "Your boy have anything to do with that mess at the Caldwells'?"

"If he did, he's not talking."

I nodded and scratched my stomach, the way Bob had. A soft breeze moved past us. I felt good. That breeze was mine once it crossed the property line. It belonged to me. I could still smell Delia on my hands and in my clothes. I was wondering if a future was possible for the two of us, and at the time, it seemed as plausible and preposterous as anything else.

I said, "Are you happy, Bob?"

"Sure," he said, matter of fact, like I'd asked him a reasonable question. "I got the wife, got the kids, got the job. I'm happy enough."

He swigged and handed me the bottle. Just the smell of it, faintly sweet and mediciney, was enough to make my stomach clench, but I muscled down another mouthful anyway. I said, "You and your wife ever have any problems?"

"How do you mean?" he said.

"I mean big stuff."

"That's a mighty personal question, my friend," he said.

"Sorry," I said. "You don't have to answer."

"It's okay." He took the bottle and drank, bubbles rising toward the bottom. He wheezed and said, "Smooooth," then capped it and handed it back. For a moment he didn't say anything, just looked toward the golf course. Someone had forgotten to bring in one of the orange flags from the green, and it flitted drowsily in the meager breeze. Bob said, "To tell the truth, there's not much in the way of big stuff. We have our troubles, sure, but nothing we can't handle. We've got a few tricks for keeping it interesting."

I looked at him. He made a devious, clacking sound with his tongue and gave me a wink. "Are you saying what I think you're saying, Bob?" I said.

"A little state trooper and the distressed motorist," he said. "A little Caesar and the emperor's wench. Never hurt anybody. The wife's got a costume. That kind of material that you think you can see through but you can't, sexy as hell. I got the hair for that Caesar action." He chuckled and tapped his head, indicating his fringe of hair. "You should see me in a toga."

"You old dog," I said.

"Hey, buddy," he said, "I was doing the slap and tickle before you were pecker-high to a Chihuahua."

I gave him a laugh. Bob was hell on the one-liners. "Look at that," he said, elbowing me and pointing with the bottle. I looked where he wanted me to look. At first, I didn't see anything, just the moonlight playing on the fairway across from us. But gradually, I picked up a shimmer of motion, then the ghost of a shape. Someone was moving around on the sixteenth fairway. I watched the figure walking back and forth, slowly, clumsily, like they couldn't see where they were going, and then I recognized her. It was Betty Fowler and her divining rod.

"She's out late tonight," Bob said.

"Crazy Betty," I said, taking the bottle when he offered.

The bourbon was kicking in, the world taking on a sort of sheen. I lay back on the yard, stretched my feet into the road. Dew was already starting to settle, tiny diamonds on the grass. Bob's wife was pretty in her way, stocky and solid, and I pictured him chasing her around the house, wiggling his fingers like a madman, saying "Give unto Caesar what is Caesar's." I laughed out loud at that, and Bob laughed too, like he knew what I was thinking. I thought of Delia at home, wondered if she could hear us out there. Above me, the sky was pricked with white stars. My father had stood with me in this very same yard and taught me the constellations. I remembered his voice, knowing and strong. I remembered his hands, one on my shoulder, the other pointing skyward. I wondered, suddenly, if he had known what he was talking about. None of the constellations looked like what he'd said they were—Andromeda, Orion's Belt, Cassiopeia. They didn't look like anything to me. Random arrangements of heavenly bodies, pale light, molten gas.

"You believe in magic, Bob?" I said.

"Like what?" he said. "Are we still talking about romance?"

"The real thing." I sat up and rubbed my face with both hands. "Spells and hexes and shit. Divining for gold."

"Let me know when you're getting ready to change the subject next time," he said. "Give me a second to prepare."

There was a split rail fence bordering the golf course and Bob walked over, loosened the drawstring on his pajama pants, and pissed on a post. On his way back, he stopped in the middle of the street, did a long look around. He said, "I'll tell you something. There's a lot of stuff in this world we don't know the first thing about. Not the first damn thing."

He slapped his round stomach affectionately, told me that he needed to be getting on to bed, and moved off in the direction of his house. He gave the garbage can one more look on his way inside.

"You never find anything in the trash," he said.

"Hope it wasn't something important."

He shook his head. "Nothing I can't live without." He started up the gently sloping driveway to his house, his slippers tapping against his heels.

I said, "Good night, Bob."

And he said, "Good night, Simon. Sleep well," his voice different all of a sudden, tender and settling, a voice accustomed to soothing nightmares.

A Diviner's Guide

Betty Fowler saw him in her sleep. There was no gunshot in her dream, just Simon falling back and away, suspended in mid-air, like a trick of levitation. Except in her dream, he never touched the ground. He hovered like mist. Betty waved the divining rod, first over his chest, then under his back, the way a magician shows that there are no strings attached. The grass pushed up beneath her feet, snaking around her ankles, her knees, her thighs, like she had been standing there for years and her life was playing itself out on time-elapsed film. In the dream, it was important that he didn't fall, because as long as he stayed above the earth, he was still alive. His arms dangled backward, his legs bent slightly at the knee, his neck curved gracefully toward the ground. He looked at her, then, dream light flickering on his face, as if through a ceiling fan, and said, "I'd like to tell you a story, Mrs. Fowler, if you have the time."

When she woke, she was dry-mouthed and agitated. She'd been troubled by the same vision every night since his death. Moonlight shifted through her curtains, drawing shadows on the wall. Her bedroom was in the back of the house, perfectly silent, far enough from the street that she didn't even have the sounds of the living world to keep her company. She wished idly that she owned a television, anything to provide a little color and distraction. Lacking that, she turned on the nightstand lamp and picked up her book and flipped to a page at random:

> To make a divining rod find a Y-shaped fork of any pliant wood, usually hazel or hawthorn. Cut the branch just below the base of the fork and grip it loosely with the ends across your palms, palms facing the sky. Hold the rod with the tip pointing horizontally away from your body. Rest your mind on the task at hand. Picture the object that you seek. See this thing floating, like a white star against a field of the deepest black, the ether of nothingness between planets. Follow your blood. Your bones know things that you don't know.

After her husband died, she had gone to the public library to research the subject, and this is what she found. *A Diviner's Guide*, cloth-backed and worn along the spine. It was still sitting on her bedside table, eight years overdue. Lizbeth Mackey down at the library had stopped calling to remind her sometime during the first year. Mrs. Fowler had promised herself that as soon as she found her husband's gold, she would return the book and pay the fines in full, no matter the cost. Every day for eight years, she had crossed the road to the golf course and walked the fairway, exactly as the book described, holding the rod with both hands, waiting for her bones to give her a sign. But neither her bones nor the divining rod had anything to tell her. Then one night not more than a month ago, she had stopped pacing long enough

to catch her breath and was standing at the fringe of the sixteenth green when she heard a voice say, "Any luck?"

She thought at first that her divining rod had learned to
speak, but the book didn't say anything about that. She
cocked her head and listened, the night full of insect noises.
She didn't hear anything else.

"Did you say something?" she asked the divining rod.

"I wondered if you were having any luck. You're out late
tonight."

She recalled another passage from *A Diviner's Guide*:

> Divining works on the level of intuition. Some experts attri-
> bute the jerking of the rod to cryptesthesia, some to divine or
> devilish inspiration, others to unconscious muscular activity,
> "sympathy," they call it, between the diviner and the object.
> One thing that is generally agreed upon is that the rod is not
> a magic talisman in itself, so much as a conduit for forces at
> work within the diviner, forces which will lead him in the di-
> rection he or she is already inclined, destined even, to go.

After a long, careful moment, she decided that, assuming
her divining rod had discovered a voice, despite the book's
certainty that it would not, it wouldn't need to ask her about
her search. It would in fact be telling her the way to go.
Warily, she opened her eyes, and there in the darkness, his
hands stuffed into his pockets, was Simon Bell.

"Are you going to hurt me?" she said.

"No, ma'am," he said. His eyes went wide and he held his
palms up between them, the way a magician shows that he
has nothing up his sleeves. "I was just curious. I was sitting
over there on the curb with Bob Robinson." He pointed back
across the street. "I was wondering how it worked, that's
all."

"There's a little girl who throws pinecones at me," she said. "One time she pushed me in the water hazard when I wasn't looking. She hides back in the trees and speaks to me in the most profane language. I don't even know what she's saying half the time."

"You know who it is?"

"No," she said. "But I'll find out."

Mrs. Fowler looked at Simon Bell, his face ashen in the moonlight. She had watched him grow up just a few doors down, had gone to the funerals of both his parents. His mother had always been kind to her, bringing around Christmas wreaths to hang on her door and inviting her to parties on the Fourth of July. His father had been a friend of her husband. The two of them would sit out on the sleeping porch and play cards now and then, or they'd just stand in the street and tell each other the lies that men told. Simon was the perfect blending of the two of them, she thought. He had his mother's narrow face and high cheekbones, his father's widow's peak and brow. She had a feeling about him, at that moment, as though they might understand something about each other, as though they shared a secret grief.

"I'll tell you what," she said. "I'll show you how it works, if you'll do something for me, too."

"What's that?" he said.

"I want you to teach me foul language," she said. "My whole life I've been going around acting like a lady. The next time that little girls speaks ill to me, I want to give her an earful she won't forget."

Now, she closed the book and walked over to the window. She could see his house, a blocky shadow against the night, could hear his voice, a distant echo of her dream. Good night, he was saying, good night. She'd always had a gift for catching the idle murmurs of the dead. Her husband still spoke to her across miles of time and space, his voice blending with the living memories of all the ghosts in the world. He'd been an amateur magician, her husband, and she had an attic full of conjurer's props—a top hat with a secret panel inside, a wand that would produce flowers at its tip—all ordered from catalogs and the back pages of magazines, simple tricks with hardly enough magic in them to fool a child. It was her husband who showed her how to make a silver dollar disappear. He'd had the idea, she thought, that somewhere in all those catalogs was a trick for making him a success again or for making the bad times vanish. She let the shade fall shut and climbed back into bed and turned out the light. Listening to the ghosts always made her tired.

Adultery
the Right Way

Delia played poker with her girlfriends on Wednesday
nights. They were all women from the apartment complex where she lived before she married Sam—Paula Dawkins,
who waited tables at the pancake house up on the highway
and Hannah Boudreau who had three kids at twenty-six and
needed to get out of the house more than any of them. Elea-
nor Wilson, a narcoleptic and the most lovely sleeper Delia
had ever seen, usually showed up. They were always having
to wake her so she could place her bets and sometimes it
seemed kinder to let her doze, her faint, musical snores like
an undiscovered instrument from some forgotten tribe. They
met at Gardenia Lawrence's dining room table. The apartment had been Delia's when her life was still her own. Now,
Gardenia had moved in from downstairs, stationed an
aquarium the size of a footlocker just inside the door, and
covered the walls with marine biology paraphernalia, shark
posters and charts outlining the mating habits of the Galapa-
gos turtle.

Delia told the women about her affair over hands of seven-card stud. She described her evenings with Simon, the way he looked at her, like he'd never seen a woman before and wanted to know all about them, and the way his hands were as rough and careless as gingham on her skin. They told her they were happy for her and that she was crazy. They reminded her of their warnings about marrying a man so much older than herself. You don't have anything in common, they'd said when she announced her intentions, these things never work out. She tried to explain, now, that her marriage was working fine, that Simon had nothing to do with some unhappiness in her life, but they just laughed and rolled their eyes and chimed whatever you say, Delia, whatever you say.

She studied her husband around the house, watched him shaving for work, considered the way he brought a fork to his lips at dinner, looking for evidence of discontent in herself, but she couldn't find anything. She loved her husband, she was sure. He still stirred an affection in her and passion, comfortable and kindhearted though it might have been. But she could walk him to the door when he left for the college, watch his car turn the corner, then slip across the driveway, her heart already thumping in dangerous anticipation, with only an occasional fluttering of remorse. It was as if she were two separate women, capable of two separate sets of emotions. She imagined that she changed shape, like in the movies, just before Simon opened the door. When she passed a mirror in his house, she half-expected to see an unfamiliar reflection in the glass.

In high school, Delia was always skipping class to go to the movies. She had been dating a boy three years older than her, and he had a car, a low-slung yellow Lincoln convertible without a muffler, and the two of them would drive into town to catch the weekday matinees. He would buy one ticket, then send her around back to the emergency exit. Once safely inside, he'd open the door for her, and they'd sit up high in the empty theater and learn the different ways they could make each other happy. The boy's teeth and lips on her neck, his hands clumsy and everywhere. She showed other boys how to sneak her into the movies after the first. What she liked the most of all, more than the sugary way they smelled or the way their shoulders would go tight when she held them in her hand, was the way the world looked when the movie was over, the surprise of heat and light and motion, like she was a magician's assistant made to reappear in a room full of spotlights.

The world looked just that way when she was with Simon, hazy and disorienting, her thighs and stomach muscles skittish from sex. Once, she was propped up in bed beside him reading a magazine in the light from the window, his fingers wandering over her stomach like he was tracing passages on a map. She closed her eyes and concentrated on the lines he was drawing on her skin, his index finger running down her leg to a scar just below her knee and suddenly she was remembering the day it happened. She saw herself in a loose gown made from bedsheets, bleary light like the light from a dream. She was headed out to the garage to show her father how she looked when she stepped on the edge of the sheet and went crashing to the hardwood floor, instantly woozy from the sight of her own blood on the fabric. She woke up in the hospital with eleven stitches threading her kneecap like the laces of a football.

"How did you get this scar?" Simon said, like he was reading her mind.

She had the strange sensation that his finger was moving past the hard white skin and touching it years back when it was still pink and raw. She had to lower the magazine and look for herself to be certain that it was healed. "I fell. I was playing dress-up and running around the house like a maniac. I was always trying to make myself look grown in those days."

He looked at her and smiled curiously.

"Wait here," he said.

She heard the footsteps on the stairs, then on the floor above her. Outside, she could hear cars flicking by on the road, the steady murmur of insects. They were sounds you stopped noticing after a while, easy enough to mistake for silence. She flipped pages in the magazine but didn't pay attention to what she was reading. When he returned, Simon was carrying a backless black evening dress with a cardboard cut-out supporting the bodice.

"Would you put it on?" he said. "I want to see how you look all grown up."

She waved a hand over her chest and said, "This is as grown up as I get," but she did as he asked, climbed out of bed and took the dress from his hands and held it against her, the silk cool against her skin. He told her the dress had belonged to his mother and she slipped it over her head, the fabric whispering secrets as it passed the length of her, then turned around so he could run the zipper up the back. She shook her hair out with her fingers.

Her own mother had always said that you could learn more about a person from their history than you could from anything they might choose to show you of themselves, and standing there in his mother's dress, she felt as if she had stepped briefly from the flow of her own life into his. He held her shoulders and walked her into the bathroom so she could see herself in the mirror. The fluorescent light showing the constellation of freckles on her chest. His face over her shoulder in the mirror. Simon had told her stories about his parents and it seemed important then to know what had happened between his mother and father, to know if this woman, whom she had never met, could have been made happy by the rest of her life. If she understood that one thing, Delia thought, it might be possible to avoid all the old mistakes of the past. She pulled the bodice up over her nose, like a bandit, and inhaled, smelling her own sweat and the soap she used and behind that a trace of dry cleaning fluid and the musty odor of disuse. Simon lifted the skirt and ran his hands along her thighs.

They spent the last hour before Sam came home going through old photo albums. Simon brought them down from upstairs and they sat cross-legged on the living room floor, flipping stiff pages. Delia would open an album on her lap and make a fuss over his baby pictures: Simon at the zoo, Simon in a sailor suit, Simon at the beach. She lingered on that one for a while, wondered if it was taken during the summer he had described for her. In the picture, Simon was running toward the camera and she could see his mother standing knee-deep in shorebreak just behind him, smiling not at the photographer but at her son. The photographer's long shadow stretched into the frame. Simon had fixed her a drink and she sipped it shallow. She asked if his father had taken the picture and he said, "I can't remember for sure, but I doubt it. Dad wasn't much of a photographer back then. Most of the pictures in here are of me and him, because Mom had to take them herself. I think she asked some guy on the beach to take this one for her."

"There were pictures of her in the first album," she said.

"That was later," he said. "Dad mellowed in his old age."

Sometimes, when Sam was at the college and she was waiting for Simon to come home from work and her own house was too quiet to bear, Delia would take the key he had given her and let herself in an hour or so early. She'd sneak upstairs and dig the albums from the back of the closet and settle on the bed. The more recent ones—Simon dressed for his high school graduation, Simon in his dorm at college, were also full of pictures of his mother, nonsense photographs showing her peeking around a shower curtain with shampoo in her hair and waving the photographer away, or coming through the front door with her keys in one hand and a bag of groceries in the other, or catching her just waking up, one hand covering her face, her nightgown rumpled, the strap hanging loose on her shoulder. And Delia imagined his father following her around with a camera, desperate to capture her, at least a part of her, on film. He could have something permanent then, something indelible and real.

But more often than not she would pore over the pictures of Simon, arrange the albums in order to watch the way he aged, showing more of his father as a baby, then his mother when he was learning to walk. It amazed her how much the two of them were intermingled in his features. He could be the spitting image of either one of them depending on the light and the angle and the expression on his face. Then he would come home, and she would put the albums away and let him draw her own memories up from her skin.

* * *

One night, she said good-bye to Simon, pulled the door closed behind her, and found a little girl standing in her driveway. The girl was twirling a baton, her back to Delia. She was eight, maybe nine years old, her hair brown, shoulder length, clean-looking but disheveled. She was wearing a man's white V-neck undershirt that reached to her knees and had cream-colored Keds on her feet. She flicked the baton skyward, and when Delia said, "Hey there," the girl turned, distracted, and the baton came clattering to the pavement.

"Who do you belong to, sweetie?"

She gave Delia a serious look and picked up the baton.

"I'm training for the Junior Miss."

"Is that right?" she said. "I know you. You're Bob Robinson's girl. You came by dressed as Miss America last Halloween. That was some costume."

She nodded and smiled, said, "You're Mrs. Holladay. Do you have another name? My mother has another name."

"Holladay is my husband's name." Delia smiled back at her, studied her face. Skinny, with high cheekbones and a round mouth. "My maiden name is Simpson."

"I like Holladay better," the girl said.

"Me, too," Delia said.

The girl smiled again and moved off in the direction of her house, crossing Simon Bell's yard, then tossed the baton into the air and followed it with her eyes. She caught it on the downward arc and kept it pinwheeling smoothly through her fingers. Delia went inside and showered away the last traces of her evening with Simon, then fixed dinner, stir-fried chicken and vegetables, and she didn't think about the girl again until her husband was home from class. They were sitting across from one another at the little table in the kitchen,

Sam poking at the peppers and onions on his plate. The table was pushed against the wall beneath the window. The window was open, warm air sighing through the screen, ruffling a basket of paper napkins.

Delia said, "Do you ever think about children anymore?"

"We've talked about that," he said. "I'm too old. You can have children with your next husband."

"Stop," she said. "I'm serious."

He said, "So am I," but his voice was soft and teasing. "The average life expectancy for a white male in the southern United States who eats too much red meat and fried chicken and occasionally smokes a cigar is seventy-one years old. I'm sixty-three now. That's eight years left to me. I want to spend them with my wife. When I'm buried and you're still fertile and alluring, you can start looking for the father of your children."

"Don't joke," she said.

Sam tried to change the subject after that, but Delia didn't have anything to say. She wasn't angry. They had talked about children before they decided to get married and agreed that they would be happier alone, no distractions. When Sam had finished his dinner and was standing at the sink rinsing dishes, she thought, No, I don't want children, then she said it out loud, "No, you're right. We shouldn't have children. It'll be just the two of us," and that sounded fit to her. She walked over to Sam and nudged him aside, told him to go into the living room. She'd finish up and be right there. A few seconds later she heard the stereo come on, something classical that she didn't recognize, extravagant with strings.

Just as she was drying the last of the dishes, a face appeared at the window, the little girl from today pressing herself against the screen. "Do I look funny?" the girl said, her voice through the mesh a brittle-sounding buzz. The screen pushed her nose flat, made her cheeks look fuzzy.

"Pretty funny," Delia said. "I thought you said you were going home. Shouldn't you be practicing your baton?"

"Ahhhhhhhhh." The girl made her voice deep, relishing the sound distortion. Then, doing a throaty Darth Vader, she said, "Luke," drawing the word out for effect, "Luke, you are not my father."

"That's not right, is it?" Delia said. "Doesn't he tell him, 'Luke, I am your father'? Isn't that the whole deal with the movie? The big surprise?"

"Some surprise," she said. "It's a stupid movie."

"I liked it," Delia said. "I don't know your name."

"My name's Maddie." The girl ducked out of sight beneath the sill. Delia could hear music from down the hall, then the low, consoling tones of the public radio announcer. She said, "You still there, Maddie? How long have you been out there listening?"

She thought she should say something about life and love and the way of adult matters, in case the girl heard something that she didn't understand. Then Maddie was at the window again, rattling the screen, startling Delia despite herself, saying, "Luke, Luke. Come to me, Luke. Come over to the dark side, my son."

The house seemed impossibly quiet that night. She lay in bed for a long time, listening to Sam breathe, because that was the only sound she could locate. She had heard that older men tended to be light sleepers, up and down all night long, but Sam generally slept like the dead, his breathing shallow and quick, like a child. After a while, she went into the other room and got the television going, flicked channels until she found a movie that she liked and pressed mute, the characters mouthing the words silently. She thought about calling Paula or Gardenia Lawrence from the poker game, but decided against it. Then she locked the door and dialed Simon's number. He answered on the first ring.

"Delia?" he said.

"How did you know it was me?"

"I have ESP," he said. "That's my thing, guessing who's calling me in the middle of the night. It's not very lucrative, but you take what you can get."

"Are you watching television?"

"I'm in bed."

"Turn the TV on. Put it on Channel Thirteen."

He sighed, and she said please. She heard him getting out of bed, imagined him in his boxer shorts, long legs ashen in the darkness, picking his way through the forest of discarded clothes on his bedroom floor to turn on the television.

"This is one of my favorite movies," she told him when he returned. "I know for a fact it'll be over in about fifteen minutes, counting commercials."

"Why don't you come over? Is Sam asleep?"

"No," she said. "I mean yes, he's asleep, but no I won't come to your house. See that guy." She pointed at the screen though she knew he couldn't see her. "He'll be dead in a second. Someone tampered with his brakes. We'll just talk until the movie's over."

He said that was okay, and she turned off the light and settled back against the couch. A bank of long windows faced the backyard, and she could see his pool, luminous in the darkness, casting scattered reflections. He was always forgetting to turn out the lights. She reminded him, and he said he'd take care of it when they were finished. It was a seven-ties' movie, and they poked fun at the Afros and fly collars and bell-bottomed pants. The house was cool and pleasant. She wanted that movie to last a long time.

The Habit of Seasons

On Halloween, Sam dressed himself as Frankenstein's Monster. Delia smeared pallid makeup on his cheeks and slicked his hair with dye and Vaseline. She lined her own mouth with black lipstick and made a witch's hat from a cardboard box, so the two of them would be appropriately scary when the Trick-or-Treaters showed. But, by and large, the children stayed away. Sam said he was sorry, he hadn't been very good about holidays in the past. When it was clear that no one else was coming, Delia piled the hem of her witch's dress in her lap and ate the leftover candy, scattering gaudy wrappers on the rug. Sam couldn't get over her knees, couldn't believe the arches of her bare feet. He leaned against the door-frame and said, "What is it that you see in me exactly?"

She smiled, lipstick on her teeth, and brushed crumbs from her dress.

"C'mere, Frankenstein," she said. "Isn't there a movie about you?"

He told her to wait a minute, went to the porch and snuffed the candle in the pumpkin. Across the street, Betty Fowler was plying her ridiculous magic on the golf course, a perfect holiday prop. He stood watching her for a few seconds, the sheen of her gray hair in the moonlight, her shadow long on the neat grass. The moon was appropriately full. Then he made his way back to the living room and made love to his wife in the dark, her kisses tasting like chocolate. He thought of Mary Youngblood and the women that followed her, marveled at the difference here, felt dizzy, almost drunk, at the pressure of Delia's knees at his side, the tickle of her hair at his face when she leaned over him, the hard floor against his back.

The seasons changed abruptly in Alabama. Winter stormed in while everyone was asleep, shaking the leaves from the trees and bringing cold November rain. They brought the extra blankets down from the linen closet. Delia drove him to work in bad weather because his eyes were going bad. One morning in December, rain streaking the hood like ice skater's tracks, the defrost working hard to keep the windshield clear, she didn't stop when they reached the high school. He asked where she was going, but she grinned and stayed mysterious, kept driving until he guessed their destination. He said, "We can't go to New Orleans, Delia, I've got a test to give. We're doing the Plebian Council and the Gracchae."

They were on the interstate, fifteen, maybe twenty minutes from town. She said he was right and turned around at the next exit, headed back the other way. The road was spitting mist. Delia's cheeks were red with cold.

"It was a good idea," she said, patting his thigh.

"Yes," he said. "It was a good idea."

A few days before Christmas, they drove out to a tree farm,

and Sam cut down a scotch pine for their house. They decorated it with lights and glass balls they had bought the same
day at the supermarket in town, and Delia strung berries to
weave along the branches. For a long time after they were
finished, they stood in the half light from the colored bulbs
with a drink and appraised the work that they had done. Some
of the berries were broken, insides seeping out onto the thread
and the ornaments looked cheap and obvious to Sam. He
said, "It takes a long time to accumulate the right stuff for a
good Christmas tree."

"I know," Delia said. "This tree is fine. It's fine. Really,
Sam, it's perfect."

She bloomed again in March, cotton dresses dancing around
her legs, preparations for the spring recital invigorating her.
She carried sheet music everywhere she went. On the night
of the performance, Sam sat in the third row beside a woman
who kept talking about her son, the cellist. That woman has
done wonders for Allister, she kept saying, he's never been
so thrilled to play his music. Sam nodded and smiled. He
knew Allister's motivation. He watched Delia, exactly the
way he'd watched her before she was his wife, her hands
waving in time to the music, her mouth circling the notes,
but instead of feeling relieved at her happiness or enchanted
at the sight of her, he felt oddly desperate and old, his limbs
heavy on his bones. He could not imagine how he had managed to live his life without her.

They surprised Delia's mother on her birthday, April 21,
brought her flowers and a microwave oven, which nearly
killed Sam when he carried it from the car. Mrs. Simpson
asked him how he liked married life and he said, "I like it
fine, Margaret. Just fine."

"Liar," she joked. She pointed at him with a last forkful of cake. "This girl's running you ragged. I can see it in your face. You've aged ten years."

Delia took her plate and slapped her mother playfully on the shoulder and said, "You shut up. Sam and I couldn't be happier."

A few weeks later, he came home from teaching his class and Delia was nowhere to be found. He knew she was probably fine, but he couldn't stop his heart from jumping to conclusions, pinballing around in his chest. He went from room to room turning on lights, calling her name, but she didn't answer. He found her on the back patio in a green and yellow swimsuit, toweling her hair, her legs and arms still slick with water. She'd been using the neighbor's pool in the afternoons. He opened the sliding glass door and said, "Lord, I've been calling you for five minutes. I thought you'd been abducted by aliens."

She smiled and rubbed the towel over her leg and said, "I'm sorry, Sam. I didn't hear a thing. My mind must have been somewhere else."

Her hair was crazy from the towel, her nipples showing through her bathing suit. Porch light glistened on her skin. Just then, he remembered what she'd said to her mother— Sam and I couldn't be happier—and he wondered if it was true. His voice was fat and mealy when he said, "Would you like me to build you a swimming pool?"

"You know we can't afford it," she said. "Simon Bell's is fine."

"I was just noticing the yard," he said. "It's empty, nothing but grass."

"That's not true. We've got the flower beds beside the house. We've got the magnolia." She pointed at the big magnolia near the fence, white flowers beginning to fold with the coming darkness. "We don't need a thing," she said, tossing the towel into his chest and kissing his cheek as she slipped past him into the house. He stood there, holding the towel, feeling the water from her body on his hands, the clammy kiss on his cheek, smelling chlorine and Delia in the fabric, until he heard the shower running in the other room.

Simple Magic

Two days after my mother's funeral, I paid a visit to her psychic. I found the address in The Yellow Pages. I never would have thought you could find a psychic in the phone book, but there it was—Madame Florence—under the heading Paranormal Services, along with about a dozen similar listings statewide, all of them Madame or Mistress somebody. She did business out of her house, which was in a hazy, gray area of town, a sort of buffer zone between the shabby neighborhoods near the waterfront and the nicer area right on the water. There was a sticker of an open black palm in one of the front windows.

"Call me Flo," she said, when she greeted me at the door.

She was a big woman, wearing a floral housecoat and bedroom slippers. A bandana was tied around her head, gypsy-style, but it was done in a lazy way, strands of wiry hair poking out on all sides, like, after all these years of telling fortunes, she had gotten tired of pretending. Madame Flo lead me into the kitchen, sat me down in a rickety aluminum folding chair, offered me wine from a jug on the table.

"Do you know who I am?" I was testing her.

"You look a little familiar," she said over her shoulder. She was getting a crystal ball down from the cabinet where it sat among all the coffee mugs and plastic cups and kitchen glasses. She shuffled over and thumped the crystal ball on the table. Madame Flo took her time settling in, pouring wine into a kitchen glass. She flipped the hem of her housecoat back and forth across her knees. She shrugged and said, "Who are you?"

"You tell me," I said.

She frowned and slumped in her chair. "Listen, if you don't know who you are, you need more help than I can give you."

"My mother was a client of yours," I said.

"I have a lot of regulars," she said. "Forty-five bucks or no more questions."

I paid, and she studied me. She drummed her fingers on the crystal ball. She said, "You are the child of Elizabeth Bell. Your name is Simon Bell. You are in college and you are twenty years old. That suit you?"

I remembered my mother's ridiculous warnings. She must have told Madame Flo all about me. Madame Flo reached across the table, told me to give her my hand. She traced the lines in my palm with a long fingernail. While she worked, she asked a few questions of her own.

"Why are you here, Simon Bell?"

I didn't have a ready answer for that. I was hoping, I supposed, that she could tell me something about my mother that I didn't already know. I didn't believe in all this hocus-pocus, hated this woman for selling it to my mother, but I thought maybe she knew something about the way my mother died or something secret about the way she lived her life. Madame Flo never took her eyes away from my hand.

I said, "I wanted to talk about my mother."

"I can't tell you anything about your mother," she said. "I can only tell you about yourself."

"What can you tell me?" I said, my voice hard.

She ran her nail along a straight crease in my hand from my pinky to my index finger. "This is your life line." She glanced at my eyes then looked away. "Yours will be a short life." She switched to the seam that curved around the pad of my thumb. Now that I was looking I could see that it wasn't a continuous line; it was broken and forked in six or eight places. "This here is your love line." She glanced at me then back at my hand. "You will know love. You'll fail before you get it right, if you ever do get it right." She tapped the heel of my hand where the line ended in skews. "This part here is a little hard to read."

I said. "That's not particularly good news."

"It shouldn't bother you," she said. "You don't believe me." She set my hand on the table, brushed my palm as if smoothing the creases from it. "Don't think you're hurting my feelings or nothing," she said. "Your momma is believer enough for the both of you."

I jerked my hand away and got to my feet.

"My mother is dead," I said.

"Oh," she said, wide-eyed. Then, after a moment, "I'm sorry. I guess you think I should have known that."

"Did you give her a date?" I was shouting all of a sudden. "Did you say when? Did you get that right?" My shoulders were trembling, my throat tight. "Did you tell her how she was going to die?"

I wanted to throw the table aside, smash her crystal ball into a million pieces, demand to know what gave her the right to deceive my mother. I hadn't come here to get angry, but I wanted to hit her now, wanted her to take the blame. She was looking at me with an expression I'd never seen on another person. She was afraid of me. And at that moment, seeing the alarm in her eyes, I was afraid as well.

"I'm sorry." She was rigid in her chair. "I didn't know."

I sucked air through my nose and counted to myself, until I had calmed a little. I apologized, emptied my wallet on the table, thirty-seven dollars, like that would make up for my outburst, then stormed outside and drove away. I kept driving until my hands stopped shaking on the wheel. Driving had always settled me. When I was a baby and couldn't sleep, my father would strap me into the car seat and tool around town, soothing me with music and gentle light and the faint vibrations of the tires on the road.

I wasn't ready to go home. Night took on a different quality in winter. The air shined. Not like summer, when the heat itself, tempered a bit by darkness, captured the light, like sheets of cellophane had been draped over every bulb in town. In February, the streetlamps were bright and unfettered and the constellations seemed closer to the ground. Driving away from the psychic's house, still reeling from all the commotion, I kept wanting to turn my windshield wipers on, clear things up a little, streaming neon and traffic lights floating drunkenly above the road.

It wasn't long before I found myself in front of Pilar's house. I knocked on the door and was greeted by an old man, his bare chest alive with wiry gray hair. Pilar didn't live there anymore. So I called this girl I knew in high school, and we swung through a McDonald's, drove out into the country and parked on the shoulder of the highway, eating cheeseburgers and looking out across the fields. Most of the farms around Sherwood grew soybeans and wind pushed through the knee-high plants, making the surface ripple like water. In the distance, I could see the blurred light of a house and a radio tower, high above everything, blinking red. I fed her french fries, my fingers coming away damp from her lips and jeweled with salt. After a while, I swung my knees out from beneath the steering wheel and kissed her, tasting grease around her mouth, and for a few minutes, we did a little dance with our hands, me working to get at the buttons of her jeans, her trying to keep me away, a tangle of busy fingers, before she gave up. This girl always gave up. She scooted her hips forward on the seat, knocking the radio dial to a news station with her heel. At some point a string of eighteen wheelers roared by, maybe ten in a row, their highbeams like flashing spotlights, and we lay together, the bland voice of the newscaster a calming whisper amid all that brightness and the deep thrum of the horns.

One time—this was before I'd moved back into my parents' house—a friend of mine, Lamont Turner, called and told me that his wife had left him. I drove over and found him sitting on a corduroy couch, his hands cupped over his knees, a green paisley necktie strapped across his eyes. A dog was sleeping in a shaded corner. A yellow Lab, gone soft from the good life, his belly round and smooth, his muzzle graying. Lamont was a writer of short stories, overly prone to melodrama.

"She wants to take the dog." He covered his eyes with his

hands, though they were already covered, then dropped them abruptly into his lap and sat up straight, saying, "Is he still here? Is the dog still here? Portnoy? You here, fella?"

The dog was sleeping in a shaded corner and thumped the floor with his tail at the sound of his name. I said, "He's found himself a cool spot. Are you okay? What can I do?"

"The light," he said, gesturing at the windows. "Ellen took all the curtains in the house. I can't stand this light."

"Okay," I said, "let's get you out of this room, first of all. There's too many windows in here. Let's get you into bed."

I went over and helped him up from the couch, one hand in his armpit, the other at his wrist. He smelled like booze and exhaustion. I thought, most likely, he'd been up all night. I just led him down the hall, one arm around his back, guided him in what felt like the right direction. I couldn't remember where the bedroom was and when I asked, he said, "She left me a note on the refrigerator. Seven years. She's got this whole time-sharing thing worked out—she'll take the dog for a week, I'll take a week. Seven fucking years."

So I just kept walking, checking doors now and then, the dog trailing behind, his toenails clicking on the floor, until I found the bedroom. I didn't know if this was the right place, but I laid him down anyway, tugged his shoes off, found a musty blanket in the closet and rigged it across the windows. He said, "I'm sorry. I couldn't think of anyone else to call."

When I lifted the blindfold from his eyes, he started crying. I let him lean his head against my shoulder, draped an uneasy arm across his back. He was a friend, after all. It made me uncomfortable to see him like this, but I didn't know anything else to do for him. After a while, I eased him back against the pillows, patted the foot of the bed so the dog would come up. I waited until he passed out, the big yellow dog dozing beside him. By the time I left, both he and Portnoy were snoring like lumberjacks.

I'd had my fair share of relationships, been with my fair share of women, but none of them had ever made it beyond the disappointments of desire. I'd gone rushing in headlong, and they had faded without much pain, like vaguely remembered dreams. There was Blair Smiley, the tax attorney, who liked to make love with her clothes on. And Bee McInerny, a veterinarian, whom I met one morning when I accidentally hit a stray dog with my car on the way to work and rushed him to the nearest clinic. We lasted three months. Her skin, even the pale insides of her thighs, smelled like flea shampoo.

There was Lucy Carver, who had a kid. A gorgeous little girl. Our first night together, we were busily doing what we could to make each other happy when her daughter appeared in the bedroom doorway, her eyes bleary with sleep, one bare foot on top of the other. I didn't think I was stepfather material at the time. In law school, there was Sue Ellen Spencer, the communist with a Southern belle's name, who wanted me to suck her toes. She was into male degradation, and I didn't mind. And Claudia Lopez, after both of us failed the bar. Four months of sad and desperate sex until we passed and suddenly had no need for one another. I'd heard she won a six-million-dollar plaintiff's verdict up in Michigan. She was a rich woman now. And gray-eyed Joyce in college. And Deborah of the cashmere sweaters, and Tuesday Martin, the only woman I had ever known who could carry on an actual conversation while making love. All of these women out there in the world with little in common except me, and still I had never known the sort of desperation that I could hear in Lamont Turner's voice. I supposed that I should have been glad about that but, strangely, I wasn't.

Now, Delia. I learned a few things about her in the time we spent together. Her teeth were slightly crooked along the bottom row. I learned that. Not so as to make her less attractive, but in such a way that she seemed more approachable, in such a way that when she smiled, it seemed almost possible that such a lovely woman could love you back. She could tie a cherry stem into a knot with her tongue and wiggle her ears. Her father left home when she was fourteen, and she never heard from him again. She was a competent piano player, not brilliant, but good enough that you would have needed a certain amount of knowledge to be able to tell the difference. I learned that, too.

My parents had a piano, though neither of them played. It was a huge white Liberace-looking number, a leftover from my father's shopping spree. Every now and then, Delia would play for me, songs that I didn't recognize, her shoulders canting almost imperceptibly to the music. Watching her play the piano, I was overcome with anxiety and longing, thinking that when the song was over, she would stand and bow, then walk out the door for good. I remembered that feeling from childhood, after we had come back from the beach and our lives were normal again. I remembered sitting on the floor beside my parents' legs, looking at movies my mother picked out, thinking that everything was fine as long as the people kept flickering on the screen. But as the good guys got closer and closer to catching the killer and the music tensed, I thought there was a chance, however small, that this simple happiness would come apart when the credits rolled, that something would go terribly and irreversibly wrong. It wasn't as clear as all that, the feeling, but no less frightening for its lack of definition.

I once asked Betty Fowler if she remembered anything about my parents, something that perhaps they hadn't told me or that I'd been too young to notice about their lives. I was visiting her almost every day by then, sitting on her porch and drinking iced tea. She'd tell me a thing or two about divining, stories about men finding their fortunes in a mountainside, armed with nothing more than a hazel branch, or she'd stand behind me and show me how to hold the rod, her palms and fingers rough as parchment on the back of my hands, and I would teach her a new swear word. The sight of her, this old woman with wrinkles etched into her skin like filigreed tattoos, pursing her lips awkwardly around the underbelly phrases of the English language, made me think of ventriloquists and comedy teams and psychic chanellers. The words were always a surprise in her little old lady's voice. "Son-of-a-bitch," she'd say, too careful and precise to be menacing, like she was repeating phrases from a foreign language tape. I liked that she still believed her husband long after any reasonable person would have given up hope, that she considered magic a sensible recourse for finding his gold. The sun would come slanting down over the golf course, throwing long shadows, bringing dust and spiderwebs to life in the corners of her porch, and it would seem possible in that moment for a person to find what he or she was looking for through the various sorceries of the heart. My father would have been uncomfortable around her, would have written her off as lunatic with loneliness and age. And, most likely, he would have been right, though I didn't want that to be the case. The day I asked Betty Fowler about my parents, she looked at me for a few seconds, considering, then said, "They were good people. They were always nice to me and Stan no matter what." Her eyes went sad and she touched my knee with her fingertips. "Have I ever told you the story about Henry Watkins and his divining rod. He was from Texas," she said. "The greatest diviner who ever lived. It says so in the *Guide*."

She held the book up with her right hand, like a testament.

Delia, however, was not so easily satisfied. She had seen two pictures of the same man in one of the old photo albums and because I couldn't identify him, she considered him a likely suspect in the search for my mother's lover. We wasted two entire evenings looking for him, slipping into restaurants like private detectives and scanning for his face among the patrons. In one of the photos, the man was standing with my mother and father on the back of a fishing boat, the three of them smiling at the camera, all decked out in summer gear. My mother was wearing a bikini, which was surprising to me for no good reason, her hips slender, her legs long and muscular, her hair wet, as though she had just come on board after a swim. In the other, my mother was sitting on the grass beside the man, both of them with their ankles crossed, plates of food on their laps, and I guessed that the occasion was one of her Fourth of July soirees. The man was handsome enough, I supposed, tall and burly with what Delia called Johnny Weissmuller shoulders. He looked about my mother's age and wore these showy shirts with broad collars and open throats. Delia carried the pictures in her purse and I half-expected her to flash them at a bartender and demand to know if he had seen this man. In my imagination, she had Mickey Spillane's voice and a hundred-dollar bill ready in her palm. To my great relief, however, we never made it much farther than the door, just lurked at the hostess station and let our eyes wander over a potential rogues' gallery of diners. She thought she saw him once, showed me the picture again—I had seen it a dozen times—and pointed out a man gassing up his car two pumps ahead of us. I had to admit that he bore a resemblance to the man in the photograph, albeit worn a bit with age, bearded now and salted with gray. At Delia's insistence, we followed him home, parked across the street from his house, and watched his windows.

"There's only one car in the driveway," Delia said. "What if he carried a torch for your mother all these years and never married? That's the saddest thing I ever heard."

"His wife is probably at the grocery store or something."

Delia said, "No, I'm almost positive that he wasn't wearing a wedding ring."

I looked at her for a long time and she looked back, managing a serious expression for a few seconds, then both of us dissolved into laughter. I said, "You couldn't possibly have seen his ring finger from where you were sitting."

"I suppose you think I'm getting carried away," she said.

"Now, you're talking," I said.

We drove home and lingered by the pool, the evening fading gradually around us. Delia eyed her watch but didn't leave. She asked me to tell her about my day at work, so I ran through a litany of research and depositions. I was telling her about a messy divorce involving an abusive wife and a husband with nine fingers when she said, "Were your parents happy? I mean after what happened. How did they manage to make everything turn out all right in the end?"

She was stretched on the lounge chair next to mine with her eyes closed, her fingers linked loosely on her stomach. The treeline was fringed with sunlight.

"You don't even know if anything happened," I said.

She turned her head and gave me an eyebrow raise, almost the exact same expression she'd worn that day on the golf course, full of pity and tenderness and surprise. My lady golfers chorused beyond the fence, doing harmony with the nimble insects and the lawn mowers up and down the street. Delia walked over and stood beside me and pushed my eyes closed with her fingertips. She sat on the edge of the chair without taking her hands from my face and lowered her head down to my chest, like she was listening to my heart. We stayed like that for what seemed like a very long time, Delia breathing against my neck, me listening while the world made itself heard around us.

Near the end of June, Sam Holladay left town for a week to go to a teacher's conference in Atlanta. Delia didn't mention the trip beforehand, just showed up at my house when he was gone and stayed for four days. She went home once in a while, of course, to pick up clean clothes or check the messages on her answering machine or to wait for Sam to call, but for the most part we were together all the time. We cooked dinner together and ate it in the dining room, silverware ticking pleasantly against our plates. Delia liked to leave the dishes in the sink, then rush off to the bedroom or the couch or anywhere there was space enough for the two of us to make love. We promised ourselves that we would get around to doing the dishes, but we never did. I liked the dirty dishes as much as anything else that week. It was like when you were a kid and your parents went out of town. You wrecked the house and everything, because there was no one around to keep an eye on you.

One evening, I came home from work and dropped my briefcase just inside the door and heard piano music coming from the living room. It was one of those overly formal rooms where no one ever actually spent time. I stood there for a minute just listening, thinking that this was what I wanted. This moment and this faint watery sound and this dim hallway. I was already taking off my tie when I came around the corner, and there was Delia on the piano bench with Bob Robinson's daughter, Maddie, beside her.

"Sorry," I said, straightening my tie. "I didn't know anyone else was here."

They swiveled around to look at me. Delia said, "I'm teaching Maddie the piano. She wants to be in the Junior Miss thing, and I think piano is a much more dignified talent than baton twirling."

"That's nice," I said.

Maddie said, "Hi, Mr. Bell. I'm not good yet."

"You've only been at it for an afternoon," Delia said. "Have a little patience, sweetie. You're a natural."

Delia tousled her hair. Maddie looked at me. "I'm a natural," she said.

"I'm sure you are a natural," I said. "But I think you better run home now. It's almost dinnertime, isn't it? Your daddy's probably worried about you."

"He isn't worried," she said. But she slipped down from the piano stool anyway and started for the door. She was wearing socks and no shoes and moved her feet across the wood floor like she was ice skating. As she was sliding around the corner, she grabbed the doorjamb and looked back at Delia and said, "Bye, Mrs. Holladay," then kept skidding down the hall until she was out of sight. Delia waved at the spot where Maddie had been. I said, "Are you crazy? She's gonna tell Bob she was here. That you were here."

"It doesn't matter," she said.

She was in a good mood, I could tell, and she didn't want me to do anything to ruin it. My mother had hung lace curtains on the windows in this room and the floor was dappled with shadow. The window was open, and I could smell a cook-out somewhere on the street. I wasn't going to make her unhappy. I sat beside her on the bench and said, "Teach me?"

"I don't do adults," she said, patting my knee. "Adults are set in their bad habits. Kids are better at learning."

That night, I sat up in bed reading over a client's will after Delia had fallen asleep. The sheet was gathered below her waist, her hip curving smoothly into the pool of light from the bedside lamp, her ribs arching toward her breasts, her arms folded in tight like she was cold, her whole body impossibly soft from sleep. I moved to cover her and she stirred, rolled toward me and threw an arm across my middle. She said something that I couldn't hear, some affectionate murmur too quiet to understand and all of a sudden I felt a weight of indefinable sadness rising up in me like a memory. I thought of the man we had spied on just a few days before, waiting out his life for my mother to love him back, thought of my mother, beautiful and young and married to a man almost twice her age. When I came home from college for her funeral, I couldn't bring myself to look closely at the body. Two of her cousins—twin sisters from Mississippi—had identified her for the police, and it seemed possible, at that moment, that they had made a mistake, that it wasn't my mother in the casket at all. She was living out her life somewhere else, with a new husband and new children. And sometimes she was afraid to fall asleep at night for fear that when she woke all the passing years would be erased, and she would find herself again in this house with a dead husband and a son in college and the burden of her own betrayal fresh and heavy in her chest.

Delia, sleeping still, shaped her hand against my thigh. I remembered my father as well, how he had managed to bend our lives back to normal, how he had managed to go on loving her, despite everything. And I wondered if a similar time was around the corner in my future, when Sam Holladay would take his wife back from me. I worried about Sam sometimes, I really did. Not that he would find us out—I wouldn't have minded being caught. Part of me wanted it to happen, in fact, wanted to have everything out in the open, clear of shadows and shame—but I worried what the discovery would do to him. He moved into the neighborhood just a year after my family. I used to cut his grass now and then when I was old enough. I'd be out doing our yard on a riding mower that my father had brought home from work and see Sam Holladay shoving a push model back and forth across the grass. He'd get caught in the tall weeds near the curb and the engine would cut out on him. He had to stop every fifteen or twenty minutes and take a break from the heat. Summer was serious business in Alabama. I'd wheel over and knock his lawn out in no time. I felt good doing it. I never asked for compensation, but sometimes he'd slip five bucks into my shirt pocket.

A few days before he left for the conference, I ran into him at the only twenty-four-hour convenience store in Sherwood. I'd gone to buy some coffee for the morning and there he was staring at the shelves of miscellaneous items, school supplies and birthday candles and toys that looked like they'd break if you even thought about touching them. He kept wringing his hands and shifting his weight from foot to foot. His hair was disheveled, like he'd come here straight from bed.

"Mr. Holladay?" I said. I couldn't help speaking to him. "Everything okay? Anything I can help you with?"

"He's been eyeballing that same merchandise for nearly an hour," the clerk said. She was in her teens with heavy black eye shadow and a safety pin through her lower lip. "You tell him I've got one finger on the alarm if he's thinking about making off with anything."

"I'm not going to rob you," he said. "I'm just not sure what I want."

"You tell him he better make up his mind in hurry," she said to me. "Else I'm calling the cops."

Sam Holladay shrugged and shook my hand.

"She won't talk to me," he said.

I said, "What brings you out this late?"

"My anniversary is tomorrow," he said. "I forgot."

"You're shopping here?"

He shrugged again and pushed his fingers through his hair, like he was just realizing how he looked. He was wearing wrinkled suit pants and his shirt was untucked. Brittle whiskers stood out on his chin.

He said, "All the other stores are closed. It's my first anniversary. I can't show up at the breakfast table empty-handed."

"Shit," I said. Then, "Oh, sorry."

A young guy in a black leather jacket and black jeans pushed the door open, making the cowbell chime, and stalked around behind the counter to the sales clerk. The two of them hunched against the cash register, whispering. At that moment, it occurred to me that I was talking to Delia's husband. Not just my childhood neighbor and the man who taught me history in eleventh grade. This was the man we'd been hiding from, the man she was betraying for me. My pulse cranked up and I could feel the hair on my arms. A light in the back of the store was blinking on and off noisily. I thought about my father and how hard it had been for him. How I'd find him lying on the couch in the middle of the night. He would tell me that it was too hot in his room or that my mother was tossing in her sleep. But I suspected that it was his proximity to her—her body a constant, awful reminder—that kept him awake. I thought, as well, about what it would be like to have an anniversary to forget, a wife to fret over in the middle of the night. I imagined Delia at home, his home, lying in his bed, the blankets gathered at her hips, her arm sprawled drowsily in the place where he had been. My house was empty and as quiet as the grave.

"What do you think?" he said, holding something up in front of me. "The set of fingernail files or the legal pad?" He laughed, sadly, to himself. "I'm screwed. How does a man forget his first anniversary?"

"Listen," I said. "Hargrove's Department Store opens at eight. You can be standing at the door when they start business and get her something nice. A dress or something. They have lots of nice things."

"A dress isn't what I had in mind for our first anniversary," he said. "I want to give her something she won't forget."

"She definitely won't forget a fingernail file," I said.

"She won't let me forget it, you mean," he said and both of us laughed.

We stood there for a minute, looking at each other, then he thanked me and walked out the door. I watched him get into the car, watched his taillights until they disappeared around the corner. I couldn't for the life of me remember why I'd come. The salesgirl said, "Now, what's your problem?" And I wondered if the man who had stolen my mother for a little while, assuming that there was such a man, was anything like me.

When I was fifteen, my father sold his company to a Dutch manufacturer who wanted to get started in the States but needed a known and respected company name to draw business. My father agreed on the condition that he be allowed to drive the Dutch tractors before the sale. He said he didn't want his name associated with an inferior product. So we went out to the acreage that Bell Tractor used for product testing and my mother and I were introduced to the Dutchman and his wife. The occasion was to be a sort of party as well, a celebration of new beginnings. There was a bar set up over by the warehouse and a swing band on the tarmac, everything arranged by the Dutch company. They had shipped over their machines, hulking bulldozers and gleaming combines and threshers, all lined up beside the field like an invading army. My father chose to test the combine first, and he asked me to ride with him. I said I'd rather not, but he insisted, so I climbed up the ladder and squeezed into the cockpit beside him. For a while, we just drove along the rows, corn falling away in our wake, my father's hands rattling on the wheel.

I said, "What will you do now, Dad?"

He looked at me a little surprised, like he hadn't considered the fact that he was going to have some time on his hands. He said, "I don't know. Your mother, she—" Then he stopped and looked at me, his eyes funny because we were sitting so close. It was the only time in my life I'd ever seen my father not know what to say. He rapped the windshield with his wedding band and shook his head. He said, "You have to do things sometimes. You'll see what I mean when you're grown. I work too hard. I don't want to lose your mother."

We kept riding for a while in silence. I didn't know what to say, didn't know anything yet, except that it scared me some to see my father like this. A world in which my father didn't know exactly what do was not a world I wanted to live anywhere near. We finished a row and made the turn back toward the warehouse where my mother and the Dutch people were waiting. A change seemed to come over my father as were were cornering to go the other way. He nudged me in the ribs and said, "Watch this," and goosed the throttle until we were rumbling along so fast I thought the combine would fly apart. My teeth shook. I could see the crowd watching us get closer and closer, their eyes going wide and uncertain when my father showed no sign of slowing down. They started backpedaling when we were maybe thirty yards away, still disbelieving, not sure that my father was about to do what it looked like he was going to do. Then we were on top of them, and they scattered, and my father kept going until he plowed into the stage, sending the band members diving for cover in their tuxedos, shoving the stage itself and all the instruments ahead of us, until finally my father cut the engine, hopped down from the cockpit, and let out the whoop of a much younger man.

"That's a fine machine, Jan," he said. "You've got yourself a deal."

After that, my father was home all the time. He wanted to spend more time with my mother and me—at least that was the reason he gave for retiring—but whenever she suggested something, a picnic or drive down to Mobile Bay, he just said no, he was tired, maybe in a couple of days.

My mother was already consulting the stars then, though not so much that it affected the way she lived her life. She read horoscopes and bought scrolled charts in line at the grocery store. She read my father's horoscope as well, looked for hints on how to handle his new inactivity, how to make him love her again.

"Look, S," she'd say. My mother always called him by his first initial. "It says that you are about to embark on a new adventure. What do you think that means?" Her voice was too happy, the way a mother speaks to a saddened child. She was still lovely, my mother.

It cheered me a little to think that he might have something new in his life, but the only adventure my father embarked on, if you could call it that, was when he bought himself a ham radio. He set it up on a card table in the attic, added sophisticated equipment to enhance his reception, then spent hours up there, talking to people all over the world. He could get towns in Southern Mexico, he said. He'd once talked to a guy in Guam. The sleek black boxes dangled wires like scuppernong vines. My father was amazed that the night could be so full of invisible, tenebrous signals.

Delia found the radio equipment when she stayed at my parents' house. I took a shower after work, and when I got out, I could hear footsteps moving above my head. I thought at first that she was just looking around on the second floor, but when I went up there, I discovered that the attic ladder had been lowered. I found her sitting on the floor listening to a guy in Hawaii talk about his pets.

"I've got a dog," he was saying, "and peacock and two goats. We got a potbellied pig that you'd get a kick out of. Boy, the kids sure love that pig. Do you have pets, Ramona?"

"Who's Ramona?" I said.

Delia grinned and pressed a finger to her lips. She whispered, "I'm using a fake name. Think of a name for yourself and you can talk to him. It's fun."

The voice said, "Come in, Ramona. Did I lose the transmission? Dammit to hell."

"No, Chuck, I'm still here," Delia said into the mouthpiece. "This is Ramona. My friend—" She paused and looked a question at me, and when I couldn't think of a name right away, she said, "My friend, De La Renta, is here now, too."

"Hey there, De La Renta," he said. "Glad to know you. You got any pets?"

"An iguana," I said. Delia was holding the mouthpiece in front of my lips. Her fingers smelled like soap. "We also have a tarantula that lives in a fish tank."

Delia laughed and rocked back on her shoulders, brought her knees up to her chest. I stretched out beside her and kissed her elbow and took the microphone from her hand. The floor was a plywood sheet that my father had carried up to cover the insulation. Chuck said, "Are you guys married?"

"Yes," I said after a second. "Almost three years now."

"That's nice," he said. "That's real nice."

Delia sat up and circled her knees with her arms. She was looking toward the round window at the apex of the ceiling, which was too smudged and dirty to see through. All I could make out were streetlights on the glass. I'd gone by to visit

Betty Fowler on my way home from work, and I thought of her then, talking to this man with a potbellied pig in Hawaii. I wondered if she was all right. If she minded too much being alone. I said, "Hey, Chuck, you believe in divining for gold?"

But before Chuck could give me his take on divining, Delia stood and flipped the switch on the radio, shutting it down, and his voice hummed into silence. She was wearing only her bra and panties, but it was hot enough in the attic that her skin was slicked with a faint layer of perspiration. She drew her hair over one shoulder and held it with both hands.

"Why did you tell him we were married?"

"I don't know," I said. "I was just pretending."

She sat in the folding chair where my father used to sit and crossed her legs. I could see a haze of dust on the balls of her feet. Her toenails were painted creamy red. I thought I'd once heard her call that color coral. She said, "My husband will be home in two days."

"I'm sorry. I shouldn't have said anything."

She nodded and twisted her hair. I heard the air conditioner bump to life somewhere in the house, but we couldn't feel it up here. Delia said, "What's she like? Mrs. Fowler, I mean."

"She's crazy," I said. "But nice enough. She thinks her husband buried a chest of gold coins in the golf course."

"I know. Sam told me the story," she said.

I walked around behind her and took the hair from her hands. She let me. I spread it on her back, then began to plait it into a braid. There was a woman once, in college, who showed me how. Over, under, across, repeat. Delia tilted her chin forward, and I played with her hair, as weightless in my fingers as fibers of spiderweb. After a while, she said, "All that wonderful technology and that guy wanted to talk about his pets."

"Funny," I said.

The Fine Art of Foul Language

From her front porch, Mrs. Fowler could see his house. In the evening, at what had been the time of Simon's regular visit, the sun would throw shaky white light against the windows and sometimes, if she let herself, she could almost mistake the light on glass for motion inside. She imagined that it had been like that for Delia and Simon, a trick of the light. They had allowed themselves to look away from their lives for a moment and the world seemed different in the peripheries of their vision, everything harmless and electric, trembling with possibility. Even now, when he came to her in her sleep, she could hear Simon saying, Funny, in this surprised, saddened little-boy voice, like he should have known better, Funny, like he should have seen it coming from a mile away.

Every afternoon, she had waited for him on her porch. They'd talk and wait for the sun to slip behind her house. Simon promised to teach her how to use profanity, but whenever she tried cursing, he'd blush and fidget in his chair. It hadn't much mattered to Mrs. Fowler whether she learned to curse or not. She enjoyed the company, particularly the company of this young man. He had a way of looking at you that made it seem as if your words were the most interesting and engaging anyone had ever spoken. His father had been the same way, leaning forward in his chair, his eyebrows raised, his watery blue eyes a premonition of his son's. She found that she couldn't keep her mouth shut around either of them.

"You know what word I like? I like that word *fuck*," she said. "I read it in a book. I think that's the filthiest-sounding word in the English language."

It was evening, Simon just off work, still wearing his tie, his jacket draped over the back of the folding chair. He laughed uncomfortably and rubbed his knees, the skin at his hairline going pink.

He said, "It's nasty all right. But I don't see how you're going to work it in the next time you hear from that little girl. It wouldn't make any sense."

"Why not?" she said. "I might say, 'You little fuck, get the hell on out of here. Leave an old woman alone.' Now, why wouldn't that make sense?"

"I suppose it's grammatically correct and everything. But you're missing the point a little. Curse words, like all the other words in the English language, have very specific meanings and implications. Just because a word is dirty, doesn't necessarily make for a quality insult."

"You should have been a college professor," she said.

"Or an attorney," he said. "Two professions equally full of . . ."

He looked at the ground and waved his hand in a circle to indicate that there was more, but he didn't say anything else.

A breeze moved across the porch making her wind chime tick like bone.

"Shit," she finished. "There's a good one."

"What? Shit?"

"Full of shit," she said. "It's a good one. With a specific implication, like you said. It's not literal. But everybody knows exactly what you mean. That one I'm familiar with."

It was getting dark beyond the screen. Streetlamps were blinking to life. Cars rolled by pushing headlights, the neighborhood settling in for the evening. Simon asked if he could turn on the table lamp, and she said that would be fine. He kept glancing over his shoulder in the direction of his house. When he left, she would close her eyes and hold his face in her mind for a long time, keep the sound of his voice in her ears. But he was still there, at that moment, even if his thoughts were somewhere else. She brushed a lock of hair back behind her ear.

"Do you need to go?" she said.

"No. This is nice," he said. "Your turn. Tell me about divining. How does it work? Better yet, what is it exactly? That's how little I know."

"Can I ask why you're interested? I'm just curious is all."

He shrugged, said, "I don't know really. I see you out there all the time. I know people sometimes still use divining to locate underground springs and whatnot. I saw this thing on PBS—it was about sorcery and witchcraft and whatever else—and they had this diviner who could find anything. I mean anything. The guy would do these parlor tricks where he'd have somebody fill three glasses with different kinds of dark liquor, right? And he'd find the scotch every time. He claimed he could even find non-physical things, like he could tell if somebody was sad or if somebody was in love. That sort of nonsense."

"Are you in love?" Betty Fowler said, not certain what made her ask.

He shrugged again, gave her a smile.

"I'm the one asking the questions around here," he said.

So she told him what she had read in the library book. How you could make a divining rod from any forked object, a coat hanger or a branch or a section of bone. Sometimes diviners didn't even use a rod, just followed the perambulations of their heart. She described how to hold the rod, your hands loosely on the ends, the shaft pointing horizontally away from your body. She explained how it was supposed to work, that often the diviner had only to stand in one place long enough before something registered in him, a tremor, a hidden pulse, like a memory of magnetic attraction, and the divining rod set about leading him where he was supposed to go. Sitting now on her front porch, the wind chime playing its familiar ghostly song, she wondered what her husband would think about her divining. He never mentioned it in her dreams. When he spoke to her at night, it was to talk about the old times, when she was young and beautiful and he was still a success and the world was all a pleasant place to live. Sometimes, faintly, she could smell his cologne on the air-conditioned breeze and she wondered if he was returning to her in the dark or if the dead just hung around this long.

All the Unsolvable Riddles

Simon had to work on his birthday. Delia woke with the sound of his alarm and watched him shuffle groggily off to the shower, then got up and made coffee for the two of them, feeling vaguely disoriented and out of place. She found herself lost in his kitchen, looking for supplies, filters and coffee cups, in the places they would have been in her house. Sam would be home tomorrow. She sat in the living room and waited for Simon to finish dressing, smiled at him when he emerged from the back of the house, his hair still wet, his fingers working his tie into a knot, and wished him a happy birthday. He kissed her and she walked him to the door. Simon was pleased with the morning and wouldn't let go of her hand. He opened the door, tried to drag her outside after him, and right then she saw Bob Robinson pitching a briefcase into his car. Bob turned to look in their direction and she wrenched the two of them back inside just in time.

She said, "Stop it, Simon. Bob Robinson is out there."

"Sorry," he said. He wiped his mouth and smoothed his tie, shifted the knot side to side on his collar. "Do I look normal?"

Delia hid behind the door when he stepped outside and closed it behind him and listened to him greeting his neighbor in the driveway, their voices pleasant enough. Both of them shouted hellos to the postman as he made his neighborhood rounds. She crept to a window along the front of the house and pushed it open just a crack so she could hear them better, Bob Robinson saying, "Maddie tells me she's learning to play the piano. Delia Holladay's teaching her. Maddie wants to be in the Junior Miss, you know."

"Is that right?" Simon said.

They were quiet for a moment and she eased the curtain back to watch them, Simon with his eyes on the ground, Bob Robinson eying Simon. Delia felt a pressure around her, the air thick, her veins going tight. She held her breath. Bob said, "I hear she's a terrific teacher. I don't know the Holladays particularly well, but I always liked Sam. He seems like a sweet old guy. Lucky bastard, wife like that."

"Yes," Simon said. "I guess so."

A dog barked down the street and both of them turned their heads in the direction of the sound. After a moment, Bob reached up and put his hand on Simon's shoulder. He said, "Don't worry, pal, you're still my favorite neighbor. You'll always be my favorite neighbor." He smiled and took his hand away and looked at Simon a moment longer, then climbed into his car and closed the door. As he was backing out of his driveway, Simon looked at his house, his eyes flicking from window to window, and Delia curled her fingers at him, though she knew he couldn't see her.

For the rest of the morning, Delia felt nervous and lightheaded. The phone rang while she was in the shower, and she nearly jumped out of her skin. She thought it might be Simon and stepped dripping onto the linoleum, then froze, afraid that it was someone else and if she answered the phone everything would be discovered. Standing there, water going cold on her bare skin, listening to the phone ring in the other room, she remembered the man they had followed home. She wrapped a towel around herself, found the pictures in her purse and checked them against her memory. It was him, she was sure. This man had known Simon's mother, had loved her perhaps. And it seemed possible that he might even know how she had managed to go on living her life despite what she had done.

Delia dressed quickly and drove across town and parked a discreet few blocks away from the house. He lived in one of the older neighborhoods down along the Arrowhead River, rows of stately homes, lawns sloping gently down to the water. She wanted to take a closer look at his house, peek between his curtains, and maybe, if the opportunity presented itself, she would find an unlocked door, a window open against the heat, and sneak inside for a look around. She knocked on the door, thinking that if the man was home, she would just ask him outright about Simon's mother, but there was no answer. She tried the knob—locked—then went from window to window along the front porch, but all of them were locked as well. Inside, she could see a dinner plate and crusted utensils scattered on the coffee table, the floor littered with magazines, and she could see a television, the old kind set back in a heavy wooden cabinet, finger marks streaked across the dust on the screen.

A little dog eyed her curiously from the sidewalk as she made her way around the side of the house. She didn't think anyone had seen her on the porch. She took off her shoes and stuffed them in her purse, then climbed up on top of the air-conditioning unit and peeked in through the window there as well. It was his room, the bed unmade, the blankets a twist of fabric on the mattress, the wallpaper yellowing with age. She could imagine how the house had looked twenty years ago, the wood floors polished and gleaming, the rugs swept and shelves dusted for when Simon's mother came to visit. The place was a wreck now, this man gradually fading into age while his house decayed around him.

She hopped down and took another look around to make sure she was unobserved, then crept around the back of the house. Just as she was turning the corner, the man stepped out of the shadows. He aimed a squeeze trigger garden hose at her like he was holding a gun and said, "Hold it right there, little lady. I've got you covered."

"It's you," she said, catching her breath. "I've been looking for you."

"What you've been doing is spying in the windows of my house," he said. "I called the police the minute I saw you coming up the walk. We're gonna wait right here until they arrive. All right? That suit you, miss?"

She followed the hose with her eyes to a spout on the side of the house, a faint mist escaping the connection and making prisms in the summer air. The man was wearing plaid Bermuda shorts and a golf shirt and leather sandals, his legs spindly and fragile-looking.

Delia said, "You don't understand. I want to talk to you. I want to ask you a few questions, if you don't mind too much. Look, I'm going to get something from my purse—it's a picture, a photograph—don't spray me, okay?"

He nodded slightly and she felt around inside the purse until she found the picture of the three of them on the boat.

He took it from her without lowering the hose. She said, "I wanted to ask you about your affair with that woman, with Elizabeth Bell. I've been seeing her son and—"

"I've never seen this woman before in my life," he said.

"But that's you in the picture," she said.

"This isn't me," he said. "It looks like me a little. I knew the other man a long time ago. That's Simon Bell, used to own the tractor plant, but I've never seen her before. This woman his wife?"

He lowered the hose and passed the photograph to Delia, pushed his glasses back up on the bridge of his nose and studied her, his eyes running her up and down. She could see the river from here, a coal barge pushing along the surface, seagulls turning circles in the air. In the distance, she could hear the whine of a motorboat. She felt vaguely queasy and slow, the air around her dense with heat.

"Are you sure?" she said, softly.

"You're a good-looking woman," he said. "You wouldn't be interested in coming inside would you? All I've got nowadays is dirty magazines. I didn't really call the police." He laughed a little, almost shyly, but Delia was already moving away from him, turning the corner and heading back toward the car, the earth shaky beneath her feet. He said, "Wait a minute, girl. I knew her. I'm remembering now. I'll tell you whatever you want to know," but Delia was gone, the little dog trailing behind her on the sidewalk, no closer to the truth than she'd been that morning.

She told Simon about the old man when he came home from work. At first, he was angry with her for going over to the house, but when he saw how saddened she was by the whole thing, he sat beside her on the couch and brushed the hair out of her eyes. Delia had stopped off at the bakery on her way home to buy him a cake, a leftover from another party that had never been claimed, with the words HAPPY B-DAY TYRONE spelled out across the top in green icing. She dipped a finger into the icing along the side and brought a dollop to her mouth. The days were impossibly long during the summer, and it was only now, at almost nine o'clock, beginning to grow dark outside. Birds were still chattering in the trees. Simon got up to turn on the kitchen light, and Delia cut two slices from the cake. He said, "What were you doing going over there? He's just some old man. He might have been armed and dangerous."

"He was only armed with a garden hose," she said. "I thought maybe he'd be able to tell us something about your mother."

"I don't care about that stuff," he said.

"Don't be ridiculous," she said. "Of course, you care. I care."

Simon sat beside her on the couch and balanced his plate on his thighs. He said, "Tell me something about yourself instead. Tell me about your first boyfriend."

She smiled at him, dipped her finger in the cake again, and touched his face, streaked icing across his cheekbone. "You're sweet to ask, but nobody can compete with first loves."

"C'mon," he said. "Tell me something."

Through a part in the curtains, Delia could see flashes of Bob Robinson's children but mostly she could hear their voices, high-pitched and excited, and the low voice of their mother. She said, "That was awful this morning."

Simon nodded and studied his fork.

"He knows, I think," Simon said. "But he won't say anything. Bob wouldn't say anything."

The children's voices swelled abruptly outside, a little desperate and anxious, in response to their mother calling them in for the night. Delia said, "It sounds like they're hunting Easter eggs or something over there."

"They sound great, don't they," he said.

Delia smiled and patted his belly. His face was flush with the last of the daylight, his tie loosened and thrown back over his shoulder like an aviator's scarf. He said, "When I was a kid, my mother would have this elaborate Easter egg hunt for me. I could never find all the eggs and she would forget where she had hidden them. My father would spend half the night cursing and waving a flashlight over the bushes, but he couldn't do any better. The yard would reek of rotten eggs for days after."

She kissed his shoulder.

"We had cats," she said. "One year, my parents decided they didn't want to get up early in the morning, so they hid the eggs the night before and our cats got into them before my brothers and I could. I remember going out in the backyard and just being devastated by the sight of these colored eggshells scattered over the grass."

She pressed her wrist to her forehead, imitating her childhood devastation. She laughed and leaned into him at the memory. They were nice memories.

"Happy Birthday, Tyrone," she said.

Her husband called from the history conference every night at nine o'clock. She would leave Simon's house and sit in her living room with a cup of coffee, waiting for the phone to ring. But on this night the call was late. Nine o'clock came and went, then nine thirty, then a quarter 'til ten. The windows went dark and Delia had to turn on a light, the room mirrored precisely in the glass. Delia had three cups and was feeling jittery from all the caffeine, and she couldn't help wondering if something had happened to her husband. She couldn't imagine what could possibly occur at an academic conference, but the worry was real all the same. Her chest felt tight, her bones watery. She checked the phone for a dial tone, then worried that he'd been trying to call at the exact moment when she had the receiver at her ear. She called the hotel, but there was no answer in Sam's room. She walked to the front of the house and looked out the windows, like she was waiting on his car and not a phone call, but she didn't see anything. Just as she was letting the curtains fall shut, the doorbell rang and Delia jumped, then took a few steps in the direction of the phone before she realized where the sound was coming from.

Maddie Robinson was standing at the door in a ballerina tutu, gold with silver sequined trim, her face made up in an amateurish way, too much eye shadow and gaudy lipstick, blush so heavy on her cheeks that she looked like she had been slapped. She said, "I thought I could wear this when I play piano at the Junior Miss."

Delia laughed and said, "Oh, Maddie, you look beautiful. Come on in. I'm waiting for a phone call. We'll work on your makeup a little."

She carried the phone back to the master bathroom and had Maddie sit in a chair at her dressing table. Maddie closed her eyes as Delia went over her cheeks and lips and eyelids with a wet cloth, her face shining and damp as the makeup came away. She looked at the two of them in the mirror, when Delia was finished, and said, "You're very pretty."

"Thank you, Maddie, so are you."

"Who are you waiting for to call you?" Maddie said.

"My husband. Here now, close your eyes so we can redo the shadow."

Maddie did as she asked, shut her eyes again and lifted her chin so that her face was to the light. There were small round bulbs outlining the mirror. Delia could feel their heat on her arms. Maddie said, "Mr. Bell, you mean?"

"No," Delia said, running an eyeliner pencil over Maddie's lids. "I don't live at Mr. Bell's house. I'm just staying there for a while."

"Who's your husband?" Maddie's eyelids fluttered like moths beneath Delia's fingers and Delia blew across them to dust away the excess color.

"His name is Sam Holladay," Delia said. She glanced at her watch. A little after ten. Then she looked at the phone. "He's a history teacher. You'll probably have him in school in a few years."

"What does he look like?" the girl said.

Right then, the phone rang and Delia dropped the eyeliner and reached across Maddie to answer it. She said, "Sam?"

"Sorry," he said. "I lost track of time. I had dinner with a guy who teaches over at the university. He was telling the funniest stories you ever heard about Catullus and Ovid and all those other lovesick Roman poets."

His voice sounded excited and far away. Delia stood and let her hand rest on top of Maddie's head. She watched Maddie admiring herself in the mirror. She said, "That sounds nice."

"It was," he said. "The lecture was good today, too."

"What was it about?" she said.

"The parallels between modern society and the state of the empire at the decline of Roman power." He made his voice bland, like he was making fun of himself, but she knew it was the sort of thing he enjoyed. "The guy was a political scientist, not a historian, but he was entertaining at least."

"Sounds like it," she said.

Maddie had the lipstick tube and was rubbing it over her mouth, making a mess, and Delia took it from her and held her chin gently in one hand, pinching the phone between her shoulder and her cheek. She pursed her lips so Maddie would know what to do, then dabbed the lipstick into place.

Sam said, "Oh come on, it sounds boring as hell. But you're nice for pretending. So, thanks."

"I'm not pretending," she said. "I like to hear you talk about history."

"Well," he said.

"I love you," she said.

She thought at first that he hadn't heard, because there was a pause and a burst of static, but then he was back. He said, "I love you, too."

They talked for a few more minutes until he said he had to go, he had an early morning, and Delia said good-bye and hung up the phone with her thumb. Maddie was waiting, making kissing faces at the mirror. She turned to look at Delia and smiled, and Delia thought for just an instant that she was going to cry. She closed her eyes and made herself be absolutely still until the feeling went away. When she opened them, the little girl was still looking at her, a confused expression on her face, and Delia pointed at the mirror and said,

"Look, Maddie. See that. That's you. That's exactly how you'll look when you're all grown up. Beautiful."

"And I can play the piano," she said.

"Yes," Delia said. "You can play the piano."

It was getting late and Delia said she thought Maddie had better be getting home. They walked outside together. Delia wanted to let Maddie leave before going back to Simon's house. Simon was expecting her. He might be getting worried, as well, but she didn't want the little girl to see her going there tonight. She watched Maddie skip across the lawn. Just as she was crossing Simon's yard, she stopped and turned back and said, "I heard a riddle today. My brother told it to me."

"What is it?" Delia said.

Maddie put both hands on top of her head, as if that might help her remember. She said, "There are three words in the English language that end in the letters g-r-y. Two of them are hungry and angry. What's the third word? I guess it isn't really a riddle. It's more just a question."

Delia put her hands in the pockets of her jeans and thought about it, running through words in her mind. She turned a slow circle in the grass. Leafy oaks, silhouetted against the sky. Dark windows on the houses across the street. The street still damp from an afternoon shower. She said, "What's the answer?"

"I don't know," Maddie said. "I thought you would know."

That night, Delia couldn't sleep. She lay in bed beside Simon and listened to night sounds drifting out of the dark like static. Maddie's riddle kept coming back to her, and she couldn't think of the solution. She considered the fact that maybe Maddie had been teasing. Maybe she had asked a question with no right answer. She closed her eyes, the sheets warm beneath her, and played the riddle over in her head for a long time—hungry, angry, hungry, angry—thinking that the answer would materialize, if she said the words enough.

Love for Beginners

I caught my mother spying on me in college. This was in November, three months after my father died, and I was sitting on the mezzanine of the student section at an Alabama football game. Bobby Humphrey had just gone over for a touchdown, bringing seventy-five thousand people to their feet, and there, two dozen rows below me, standing perfectly still among all the bellowing fans, was my mother. She was wearing a white woolen overcoat, her hands stuffed into the big pockets, and her cheeks were red from the cold. She was smiling, watching me through the crowd. I left my date and went trotting down the stairs, but when I reached the spot where she'd been standing, my mother was gone, vanished into the crowd like a hallucination.

Later, as I walked home along Bear Bryant Drive that night, too drunk to be aware of the cold, her car came easing up beside me and she pushed the passenger door open and told me to get in before I froze to death. She had a cigarette in one hand, a pencil line of smoke trailing up from between her knuckles. I said, "What are you doing here, Mom?"

"You drink too much," she said. "I saw you in that bar."

"You were at the bar?" I said. "Jesus, Mom. I don't drink too much and you didn't answer my question. You shouldn't be spying on me anyway."

We were idling slowly beside the curb and she stopped the car, kept her eyes ahead of us like she was looking for something. Old oak trees loomed in the darkness, their branches bare. "I just wanted to make sure you were all right," she said. "That's all." She took a drag from her cigarette, let the smoke trail wistfully up from between her lips.

I said, "That's another thing. You don't smoke."

She smiled, took my hand and held it between hers. She said, "Your mother is full of surprises, Simon. There's a lot you don't know about your mother."

"Are you drunk?" I said. "You're acting very, very weird."

"A little," she said. "I had to stand in that bar for hours."

I laughed and took my hand back and propped my feet up on the dash. The heater and our talking made the windshield mist over. Every now and then, a group of students would go stumbling past on the sidewalk, their voices like a burst of color, their shoulders bumping all the way. The sky was crazy with stars. I shook my head and said, "My mother is drunk. Does this have something to do with that psychic lady?"

"I was just worried about you, that's all," she said.

"I'm fine. There's no need for you to worry. I'm fine, okay?"

She pulled the gear shift back down into drive and we rolled forward again, making our lazy progress through campus. Alabama had come from behind to beat LSU that day and everywhere you looked were the trappings of celebration, streamers of toilet paper in the trees, empty bottles beside the road, bits of crepe paper from torn banners blowing across the wintry lawns. My mother asked if I would mind driving around with her for a little while before she went back to her hotel and I said that was okay with me. She told me about Madame Florence and her connection to the other world, reminded me that I should be more polite to my dates. We never left campus, just cruised past the fraternity houses, still lit and still loud, even at this hour, and past the stadium, where RVs were parked in long rows like military barracks, humming quietly in the darkness. I said, "Are you okay, Mom? You're going through those cigarettes." And she said that she was fine, too, she just missed my father. There were a few things she had wanted to tell him before he died and for some reason Madame Florence was having trouble channeling his ghost.

I saw her again at Christmas, but she was the lady I remembered this time, no smoking or mysterious behavior or spying on me late at night. She tried hard over the break to live up to my idea of her. We trimmed the tree and stood at the windows on Christmas Eve to watch all the neighborhood men gather at the curb with a drink and commiserate about the missing pieces of toys and batteries not being included. "Your father used to stand out there with them," she said, "but he never really felt a part of things. He was older than most of the fathers around here."

I had made each of us a martini and was feeling very mature with my alcohol and my grief. Beyond the window, Christmas lights were strung along the eaves of houses; there were even strings of white lights in a few of the evergreens along the golf course, all of them combining to make the neighborhood look vaguely unreal, something you might see in a magazine advertisement.

"You can never plan what will happen in your life," she said. "Your father didn't understand that some things are beyond your control." She pointed out the window like what she was talking about was somewhere out there. "Have you ever been in love, Simon? You don't have to answer if it makes you uncomfortable talking to your mother about this."

"I don't think so," I said.

"Well," she said. "That's okay, too."

An hour or so later she fell asleep on the couch, and I covered her with a quilt when I couldn't wake her. I stayed awake for long time, sat on the floor beside her and watched the fire dance in the fireplace. I'd never stayed up this late on Christmas Eve, and it was nice to be there in my quiet house. I wrapped my mother's presents and put them beneath the tree, doing a little Santa Claus impersonation of my own.

Just before I went to bed, I walked back to the front of the house and looked out the windows again. The men were gone, finishing up their last-minute preparations. Across the road, lit faintly by the strings of lights, was Betty Fowler, searching diligently, even on Christmas Eve, for the gold her husband had promised. He died my first year of college, and I couldn't remember him at all that night, couldn't call his face to mind or even remember a single occasion on which we'd spoken, though I was sure we must have, since I'd lived a few doors down from them my whole life. I had no idea then, standing at the window of my parents' house, that I would be out there with her years later, receiving lessons from her on how to find a thing which more than likely did not exist. She would stand to one side while I made my clumsy way along the course, holding the rod in my hands per instruction. Since I had nothing to look for of my own, she had

me focus on her husband's gold, told me to imagine a minia-
ture mahogany chest, filled with gold coins, pirate coins, she
said. Fucking doubloons.

On the third day of July, the same day Sam Holladay was
to return from his conference, Betty Fowler asked me to re-
vise her will. She came by my office and handed the evidence of her existence across my desk: the deed to her house,
an inventory of material possessions, what was left of her
husband's investment portfolio. She had a copy of the most
recent draft—there had been several, it seemed—and I noticed on the second page that she had bequeathed a chest of
gold coins to a someone named Grapefruit Wilkins.

"Is this the gold on the golf course?" I said.

"It is," she said. "That's what I want to change."

I started to tell her that, for estate tax reasons, she couldn't
claim something that she wasn't even sure existed, but I figured that the previous attorney had probably felt sorry for
her and let her list it anyway. She didn't have dependents
who would be burdened with untangling the tax code. She
didn't have anyone and that seemed to me reason enough to
go along with the charade. She was wearing a Sunday dress,
midnight-blue and shapeless, a strand of pearls looped twice
around her neck. There was a window behind my desk, rain
tapping against the glass, and I stood to pull the shade.

"Who's Grapefruit Wilkins?" I said.

She said, "He's a gospel singer out of Tuscaloosa. It was
just this crazy idea I had to leave the gold to him. I saw him
on television one time."

"What made you change your mind?" I said.

"Well," she said, smoothing her dress across her thighs,
"there's someone else I'd like to give it to now."

"Who's that?"

"I want you to have it," she said. "I'm bound to find it eventually, and if I don't then you'll know how to look."

I cleared my throat, pushed my fingers through my hair. I walked around my desk and sat beside Betty Fowler on the couch. I said, "Mrs. Fowler, I appreciate the thought. I really do. But I can't let you change your will for me. There's legal propriety to think about, for one thing. How would it look for me to write myself in for such a generous gift? Plus, I just don't feel right about accepting something your husband meant for you."

"I'll find another attorney then," she said. "I mean for you to have it."

She put her hand on my knee, tugged at the fabric of my suit pants. She was looking at my tie. I had this globe that had stood in my father's office, the kind with misshapen continents and painted-on sea monsters, and I gave it a spin, let it go around a few times before stopping it with my finger.

"I'll tell you what. Why don't we just leave it out for now? We'll know that it's there and what you intend for it. There doesn't seem to me any reason to go to all the trouble of making it official. We'll know."

"You'll take it if we do it that way?"

"Yes," I said. "Anything you want. Thank you."

"All right," she said.

We stood, and I offered her my hand, but she leaned in and kissed me on the cheek, her mouth warm and whiskery. She drew back and rubbed my jawbone with her thumb, saying, "Lipstick." She looked at me for a moment, then gave my face a final scrub before heading off down the hall and out the door and into the weather, using her umbrella like a cane.

* * *

The same rain that sent me home early from work, because the power kept blinking out and the computers went
on the fritz, stranded Sam Holladay at the Atlanta airport. It
was one of those summer thunderstorms that blew inland
from the Gulf of Mexico, choking gutters and rattling windows. Air traffic was backed up all over the southeast, and
Delia told me Sam wouldn't be able to get home until the
weather service okayed the skies. Delia asked me to come
over and help her clean the house for his arrival. I vacuumed
while she put clean sheets on the bed; I dusted in the bedroom while Delia wiped the kitchen counter. We were mostly
quiet, the end of our week together hanging in the air like
smoke. When she was finished in the kitchen, we sat on the
floor of her bedroom and played Crazy Eights by candle-
light, because the power had gone out again.

Delia said, "What do you think of me, Simon?"

"How do you mean?" I said. "I love you, if that's what
you mean."

I said the words without thinking and they felt surprising
in my mouth, almost as if they had a taste. Delia played an
eight, changing the suit to clubs, which she knew I didn't
have. I had to draw cards until my hand was fat as a paper-
back book. My fingers were shaking. Delia looked at me for
a long moment over the top of her cards. She said, "That's
not what I mean and you're not in love with me anyway. I
mean what sort of woman do you think I am? Sitting here
with you while my husband is stranded in the rain at some
godforsaken airport."

"I do love you," I said, too loud this time.

"Please, Simon," she said. "How could you possibly be in
love with a woman like me? For the twenty-seventh time in

a month, I'm about to have sex with a man who isn't my husband. We are about to have sex, aren't we?"

"I hope so." I tried a smile. "Is that how many times really?"

"I don't know," she said.

Rain tapped the roof, the muted sound of drumming fingers. I'd been in her bedroom before, but only once, the first time we were together, and it surprised me to see so many signs of her husband here. His trousers draped across the back of a chair, a belt still slung through the loops. Change on the dresser top that I could imagine him scattering when he came home from work. Delia always seemed completely her own person to me, unattached to anyone, but she was here as well in the form of hair on the pillowcase and dresses in the closet and makeup and perfume on the dressing table in the bathroom.

She said, "I don't want you to be in love with me, Simon. I don't think you are, but just in case, let me remind you about that man from the other day. He was the saddest man I have ever seen. That's what happens when you fall in love with a married woman. You get all broken up and read dirty magazines and say lewd things to young women. He was pathetic."

"I thought he wasn't the right guy," I said. "Maybe he was lewd and pathetic from the day he was born. He didn't even know my mother."

"Regardless," she said. "It's nice of you say something like that to make me feel better, but let me assure that you are not in love with me, okay?" She played her last card, folded the deck back into a perfect rectangle and stuffed it into its box, then stood and began unbuttoning her blouse.

"You may have some feelings for me, but they aren't what you think."

"They're not?" I said.

"No," she said, tugging her shirttail from her jeans to get at the bottom few buttons, showing me her bra and the freckled skin at her chest. She was standing with one foot on top of the other, her toes curled under. "They can't be. I'm in love with my husband."

"And I'm in love with you," I said.

"No, you're not," she said. "Pay attention."

She smiled sadly and let her shirt fall backward from her shoulders, down her arms, the fabric gathering at her heels. I could feel the blood in my neck and fingertips. She pushed her hair out of her face and held it back for a moment, the candles drawing shadows on her skin like writing in an ancient language.

She said, "Tell me that you don't love me. It'll just make things too complicated. Say it, please. It will make me feel better to hear you say it."

"I can't say that. It wouldn't be true."

I stood and took a step toward her, but she took a step away. She undid the top button of her jeans and pulled the zipper down, and I could make out the lace waistband of light blue panties. She said, "I'm serious, Simon. We cannot be in love. It'll be too hard. I keep thinking about that little girl."

"Maddie Robinson?" I said. "What about her?"

"She doesn't know that I'm a bad person."

"You're not a bad person," I said.

She raised her eyebrows and said, "Look at me."

The windows were blurred with rain, making everything wavery and slow like we were at the bottom of a swimming pool. She slipped her jeans down her legs and stepped free. I was having trouble catching my breath. She said, "Tell me, Simon. My husband will be home soon. I want to hear you say it." Her lips were on my neck, her hands pushing across my chest, and I said, "I don't love you. I don't," and I didn't know whether or not I was telling her the truth.

Valium and Aviation

Sam Holladay was afraid of flying—he didn't see the inside of an airplane until he was forty-one years old—and he supposed it showed because the woman beside him on the flight from Atlanta touched his arm and said, "Sir, would you like a Valium? You look a little worried. I never get on a plane unless I'm free and easy." She was in her mid-twenties, blonde and going to fat. A baby was sleeping quietly on her lap. She smiled and motioned toward her purse. "I'd be happy to share. The baby only had a quarter tablet and look at her."

He shook his head and returned to the window, watched lightning flicker in the clouds below them, rain streak the Plexiglas. It was a commuter plane, fourteen seats, propeller driven, and it dipped and shuddered constantly, his stomach falling down and away and up again. He gripped the armrest and clenched his teeth. A psychologist friend had told him to think pleasant thoughts so he called his wife to mind: Delia with a towel wrapped around her head, her foot propped on the coffee table so she could paint her toenails. He had told her not to worry about picking him up—his car was already at the airport and besides, he hadn't known for certain when they would be cleared to leave—but now he wished that she was going to be waiting there, scanning the deplaning passengers for his face.

The plane bucked beneath them, sending his heart into his throat, and the woman giggled like she was on a carnival ride. He said, "On second thought," and smiled at her and held out his hand. He waited while she searched her purse, then swallowed two tablets dry. She patted his arm and gave him a dreamy look and told him that everything was going to be fine.

She was right. By the time they touched down, Sam was feeling vaguely weightless and likable and everything looked slightly off-kilter to his eyes, like he had seen these things before, the baggage claim carousel, his old Cadillac, the cows asleep on their feet along the road to town, but he couldn't quite remember when or where. He tapped the steering wheel in time to the windshield wipers, like they were playing jazz. He drove past his own house, realized his mistake and attempted a reverse entry into the driveway, knocking over his trash cans and drawing Delia out front with all the noise. She trotted over and opened his door. When he stepped grinning from the car, she said, "My Lord, are you high? You look like the cat who swallowed the canary."

"Quite," he said, leaning in to kiss her, missing by an inch or two and planting his lips against her eye. "A woman gave me Valium on the plane."

Delia laughed and led him inside, got his shoes off and

situated him on the bed. She made pancakes, brought them back to him and they ate until their cheeks were sticky with syrup. Sam said, "I had big plans to ravish you, but I'm mostly just tired now."

"That's a shame," she said. "You haven't ravished me in months."

She fingered the bedspread, and Sam thought he detected a note of genuine sadness in her voice. She was wearing checked satin jogging shorts and he ran his hand along the smoothness of her thigh, rolled to kiss her breast through her T-shirt. She held his head against her chest. She said, "Soon, okay. But not tonight. You go ahead and sleep."

He shifted his head into her lap, and she ran her fingers through his hair. He could feel a pulse between them but he couldn't tell if was his or hers.

He said, "I'll do anything to make you happy."

"I know," she said.

"Sometimes I think I'm losing you already," he said.

"You're wasted," she said, brushing her knuckles along his cheek.

"I won't lose you, Delia."

He wanted to tell her about the first night of the conference when he couldn't sleep and called her after midnight. He had wanted to say that he missed her very much and that he was thinking of her all the time, even when he was forgetting to rinse his whiskers from the bathroom sink, even when she had to be reminded that her husband was too old to be a father. He was thinking of her, that was all. But when he called, he'd let the phone ring forever, and she wasn't home. He kept calling until morning was showing itself against the windows, anger and panic building in him in equal measure—that's what he wanted to tell her—but now, with her soft hands in his hair and her pulse tapping faintly against the side of his head, all of that seemed impossibly far away.

Part 3

And it seemed as though in a little while the solution would be found, and then a new and glorious life would begin; and it was clear to both of them that the end was still far off, and that what was to be most complicated and difficult for them was only just beginning.

—Anton Chekhov

Independence Day

Every Fourth of July, the Speaking Pines Country Club put on a fireworks display. I didn't want to go to the party alone, but Delia was going to be there with her husband. My intention wasn't to cause trouble. I had the idea that I would stand in the background and watch her moving through the crowd, the careless glimmer of bottle rockets and Roman candles lighting her upturned face.

That afternoon, I hauled my father's riding mower out from the garage and leveled the grass, the sun in my face, then on my neck, as I made the rounds. The sight of a newly mowed lawn always made me feel good, like if a man could assert his will over nature, even so insignificant a thing as crabgrass, neaten and shape it as he pleased, then it might just be possible to do the same thing with his life. When I was finished, I went inside and tried to nap but thoughts of the party kept me from losing myself entirely in sleep. I gave up after a while and hit the shower, shaved with the water beating against my back, then spent an hour trying to decide what to wear.

The clubhouse was set back away from the road, built as a sort of centerpiece for the neighborhood, all faux antebellum, fluted columns and hitching posts for horses that would never arrive. An immense American flag was hung above the entryway. There was a knot of women just inside the door, my lady golfers all, their voices as familiar to me as old songs. I pushed through the crowd, weaving in and out beneath patriotic bunting and smaller flags on wooden sticks tucked into potted plants. In the ballroom, the band was playing a Wilson Pickett song.

I found Delia and Sam in the club dining room. She was wearing a plain, cream linen dress, lighter than her skin, and her hair was tied back with a burgundy ribbon. She noticed me looking at her and curled her fingers, giving me a private smile, her shy mouth working a bite of food, and it made me feel unexpectedly pleased to have this secret between us. The secret was ours alone and that was at least something.

The fireworks weren't scheduled to begin until ten o'clock. There were two hours to kill, so I got a drink at the bar and walked out onto the back patio, which faced the golf course. I watched a group of children playing on the putting green. The sun was clinging to the horizon, bands of light pushing weakly through the trees. The kids were all dressed for the occasion, the girls in cotton dresses, the very young boys in those shorts-jumpers with embroidered collars that were such an embarrassment when you saw pictures of yourself wearing them as a child. Bob Robinson found me out there. He sidled up and said, "I told her not to get dirty. Her mother's going to kick my ass for those grass stains." He pointed at the children, and I picked Maddie out in the group.

"She's a beauty," I said, still feeling a little awkward from our last meeting.

He shook his head and said, "She's gonna be trouble. Look at her bossing those boys around." He paused and we watched Maddie organize four or five young boys into a seated circle, then walk around touching the tops of their heads. Her voice was faint and musical. "I wake up in the middle of the night thinking about the day one of those sons a bitches shows up at my doorstep with flowers in his hand and a hard-on in his pants. I swear to God."

Right then one of the boys jumped up and began chasing Maddie around and around the circle. I could feel Bob stop himself from going out there. He reached into the breast pocket of his blazer, brought out a silver flask, and wheezed when he took a sip. I wanted to reassure him somehow that I was on the up and up, still on the same side of things as all the other decent people in the world.

"She's a good kid, Bob," I said.

"She'd be a better kid if I stuck her in a convent for about thirty years," he said. "She's already more trouble than my boys. You remember we talked about the toilet paper over in the Caldwells' trees. That was her. She's got this broken lock on her window, and she just lets herself in and out as she pleases. I tried to fix it, but it's an old house."

"I wouldn't worry too much."

Bob took another swig and said, "Whatcha got in there—bourbon?" When I said I did, he poured some of his whiskey in my glass. "You need to stay on your toes at these shindigs. They can be deadly."

Maddie saw her father and trotted over and Bob tucked the flask in his jacket. She said, "What are you talking about? Grown-up stuff?"

"What we are talking about, honey," Bob teased, his voice full of aching adoration, "is what a pain in the ass you are. We think you should go to a convent and become a nun. What do you think?"

He crouched so he was eye level with her. She made a face at him and said, "I don't want to be a nun, Daddy. I want to go down to the duck pond with everybody else. Can I go, please?"

"Why don't you stay here and dance with your old man?"

She stood between his knees and circled her arms around his neck and kissed his cheek. "We can dance at home. I have to go now." She kissed him a second time.

"See what I mean," Bob said to me. "I can't win. She's working the voodoo already." Then to Maddie, "How old are you?"

"Daddy," she said, shocked. "I'm nine. You know that."

"Nine years old," he said. "You believe it? Working the voodoo magic at nine years old. This one's gonna break my heart."

When she was gone, Bob and I walked inside. There was an oldies band playing in the ballroom and six or eight couples dancing at the base of the stage. Bob found his wife in a conversation with Louise Caldwell, and tugged her away to dance while she muttered apologies over her shoulder. I didn't see Delia anywhere. Soft-footed waiters made the rounds carrying drinks. The air was a jumble of voices. I was thinking, suddenly, about Betty Fowler. I was sure that she could hear the music from her house. There was nothing more lonely than distant music. I thought of her in my office, thought maybe I'd duck away from the party for a few minutes and pay her a visit. I did a quick tour of the party looking for Delia and, when I couldn't find her, slipped out the front door and made my way down the street.

The road was dark, the clubhouse a dim glow behind the trees. The porch light came on while I waited. Betty Fowler answered the door in a robe and slippers and looked surprised to see me standing there.

I said, "Good evening, Mrs. Fowler. I was hoping you might want to dance."

"Oh, Simon," she said, touching her hair, smoothing her hands along the sides of her robe. "Don't be silly. I'm a mess. I can't dance with you."

"What you mean to say—I think—is, 'I look like shit,' which you most certainly do not, and 'I can't dance with you, goddammit,' which you most certainly can. Please," I said. "We'll dance right here on the porch. I would consider it an honor."

"Well," she said. "All right. Asshole."

She smiled and let me put an arm around her back. We could barely hear the music, just the shiver of it on the air. She rested her head on my shoulder and we turned slow circles on the porch. Her hand was cool and dry in mine, her breath warm against my neck. She said, "You're sweet to do this."

"I was bored silly at the party," I said.

"I danced with your father once," she said. I waited for her to go on, but she didn't say anything else. Our feet whispered on the wood planks.

I said, "You're a good dancer."

"So are you," she said.

At some point, the music changed on us. I could hear bass now and the rattle of cymbals, a faster song, but we kept to our leisurely rhythm. I closed my eyes and settled my cheek on the top of her head. She was at least a foot shorter than me, and I had to stoop to reach her, but I didn't mind. There was an assurance to the way she moved, the confidence of many dances past.

Amateur Astrology

Delia danced a jitterbug with her husband. He moved slowly on his bones and she found herself wondering where Simon had gone. She'd just seen him a half hour before when she was eating dinner. Then she felt guilty about letting herself think that way. She remembered how Sam had grown forlorn the night before, how he had fallen asleep with his head in her lap, then waved his sadness away the next morning, blamed it on Valium and exhaustion. She poured herself into the dancing now, sliding through Sam's legs on the hardwood, spinning fast beneath his hand, her dress blossoming around her thighs. And Sam wasn't really such a bad dancer. He had a certain grace, a casual aplomb. When she was a girl, her father had twirled her to Chubby Checker records in their front yard, fireflies making a string of lights in the trees, and she remembered all the old steps. The rest of the dancers made room for them on the floor. When the song was finished everyone applauded, and the singer said, "Let's hear it for the flashiest couple in the house."

"I'm about to have a heart attack," Sam whispered in her ear.

She kissed his cheek and said, "We'll get some air."

They made their way out to the patio, walked away from the crowd to stand over by the pool. It was a perfect silver slate in the intermediate light. Across the water, she could see teenagers in deck chairs smoking cigarettes. Sam took a deep breath and said, "My God. My heart's kicking like a mule."

"Are you okay?" she said, giving his hand a squeeze. "Do you want to sit?"

"I'm fine," he said. "I'll be fine now."

He put his arm around her and drew her against him. He laughed lightly to himself—about what, she didn't know—and let his fingers trace the line of her bare shoulder. She was feeling oddly disconnected, as if she were seeing herself from a great distance or watching herself in a movie. She had the sense that she should be urgently ashamed for what she had done to her husband or that something should have changed between them, but nothing had that she could tell. She stood in almost this same spot on this very same occasion last year—just a few weeks after their wedding—and felt almost exactly as she did now. Affectionate, vaguely blessed, serene. She liked the warmth of his rib cage and she remembered thinking that his heavy arm would make a buffer against whatever bad things might happen in her life. She thought nothing could crawl out of the darkness and find her there. And nothing ever did.

She said, "Do you remember telling me that we were nearing the end of the world as we know it? That you were getting a serious late-Roman Empire vibe and we were headed for a fall?"

"I remember," he said. "You were in the tub."

"Well," she said. "It isn't true."

"It's not?"

"No," she said. "Ours will be remembered as a golden age."

"I'm glad," he said.

He hugged her against his ribs and laughed a little. She could feel his heart racing beneath his shirt. She lifted her face and kissed the underside of his chin.

"Thank you," he said.

She said, "My pleasure."

Just then, she heard footsteps clattering on the flagstones and saw Maddie Robinson laughing hard and racing in her direction. Her father was in hot pursuit, flexing his fingers in a playfully menacing way. Maddie ducked in between the two of them and said, "Mrs. Holladay—Mrs. Holladay, tell him to let me go down to the golf course and watch the fireworks with everybody else."

Her father came panting up—Delia could smell whiskey on his breath—and said, "Can you blame a dad for wanting to spend some time with his girl? Maddie, let go of Mrs. Holladay's dress. You don't want her to get all wrinkled like your old man." He bent over and put his hands on his knees, breathing hard. "Hi Sam, by the way. Hello, Delia. It's nice to see you here tonight."

Delia said to Maddie, "You should do what your father says."

"I don't want to watch with him," she said. "I want to watch with you."

"These nice people don't need to be bothered by little girls," Bob said, grinning, clearly proud of his daughter. "C'mon, I'll buy you a pop at the bar."

"Will you take me down to the golf course? He'll let me go if I'm with you, I bet." Maddie looked at Delia with pleading eyes.

Delia glanced at Bob, who shrugged, then at Sam, who said, "You go ahead. Bob and I will stand right here and talk about the reign of Caligula and the last days of Roman influence."

Delia smiled and touched his arm. Maddie took her hand. As they were making their way out onto the course, she heard Bob Robinson say, "What the hell're you talking about? I thought Caligula was the name of a titty bar chain."

Delia took off her shoes and followed Maddie into the dark, music and voices fading behind them. Pine trees rose up quietly in the warm night, and Delia could feel a band of sweat on her upper lip. After they had passed a second set of tees without seeing anyone else, Delia said, "Where is everybody?"

"I don't know," Maddie said. "They told me they'd be out here."

"Who told you?"

"They did," she said. "The rest of the kids."

Delia stopped and looked around. She had the feeling for a second that she was being led into an embarrassing trap, like a surprise party or *Candid Camera*, but she couldn't see anyone in the rough. She thought about her husband alone with Bob Robinson, wondered what if anything Maddie's father knew for sure. It was a clear night, the sky riddled with stars. She said, "Well, the fireworks are going to start any minute. Should we just watch from here?"

"Okay." Maddie sounded pleased.

"I'll tell you what we'll do. The fireworks are gonna come up over those trees," she said, pointing toward the clubhouse. "We'll lie in the grass." She stretched out, her feet facing the party. "And they'll be right over our heads. You won't be able to see them leaving the ground. It'll be like magic."

Maddie lay down beside her and took her hand. They watched the galaxies turning in the sky. Delia found herself thinking about Simon a second time, his face swimming up behind her eyes like a helium balloon. She could almost sense him nearby. His warmth and breath and the calluses on his fingers. She tried to imagine what her life would have been like if they had never met, called up the day she helped him unload his luggage from the car, then the day she'd found him following her on the golf course, and tried to rub them from her memory like markings on chalkboard. But she couldn't do it. She could not imagine her life without his imprint on it. They had done what they had done, and she did not want to be sorry. The wind rustled in the trees. This beautiful little girl was lying on the grass beside her, looking at the stars, and she felt light-headed at the turn her life had taken. Like she had two lives, two skins and hearts.

"Do you know the names of the stars?" Maddie said.

"Some of them," Delia said. "I used to know them, anyway."

Maddie pointed and said, "That one, those three there?"

"That's Fatty the Magic Pig," Delia said. "And the next one to the right is Smokey the Bear. He's the fire guy. He wears a hardhat and blue jeans and goes around saying, 'Only you can prevent forest fires.' " She made her voice deep and bear-like. "You've never heard of Smokey the Bear?"

'I think I saw him on television," Maddie said.

"He's a celebrity," Delia said, "Everything in the world is named after a celebrity nowadays." She closed her eyes and let the night wash over her, Simon and Sam and the nameless future. Without looking, she said, "You see that dark spot on the moon? It's sort of bluish. That used to be called the Sea of Tranquillity, but now they call it the Sea of Al Pacino."

"You're joking," Maddie said.

"You're right," Delia said. "Whatever you do, don't listen to me."

Reading the Signs

On my way back to the party, I found a wristwatch lying in the grass on the golf course side of the road, moonlight catching on its face, the hands turning toward ten o'clock. I hadn't wanted to go back at all, but Betty Fowler insisted. She said if I stayed another minute, she'd start to cry, which I didn't understand. I could still feel the terry cloth of her robe beneath my hand, could still smell the powdery way she smelled. I felt good, oddly content, as though something were going to happen soon, and I was ready for whatever it might be.

I stooped to pick the watch up, weighed it in my hand. It was a bulky, metallic number, the face white with Roman numeral digits. Dew was beaded on the glass. I was thinking of a girl I used to know who went around wearing men's clothes all the time, pin-striped suits and fedoras and dinner jackets—she used to have a watch like this—and right then I heard voices coming from the fairway. I held my breath and listened.

"What's that one?"

"That's Oprah, The Patron Saint of Lovelorn Women. Are you lovelorn, Maddie? Do you have a boyfriend?"

Delia, her voice light and amused. I crept over the fence and through the knee-high grass and went slinking from tree to tree until I could see them—she was with the little girl, Maddie Robinson—lying side by side in the grass. Maddie said she didn't think she was lovelorn, then laughed and fidgeted toward Delia like she wanted to get closer. Delia with her hands behind her head, her eyes on the stars. The moonlight made a patina on their skin, and I thought that this was the most beautiful thing I had ever seen, the two of them etched against the silvery grass. I wanted to stay hidden and watch them, the night fading into the background.

"Did you hear something?" Delia said.

I held my breath again, my heart beating in my stomach and behind my eyes. I pulled myself tight against a tree, the bark biting my cheek. Delia sat up and looked in my direction.

"I think I heard something, Maddie. Maybe we should be going."

"No, I like it here," she said. "Teach me another one."

I didn't want Delia to worry, so I stepped out from my hiding place and held my hands out, palms up in surrender. Delia laughed and touched a hand to her chest and said, "Simon? Jesus." She put her finger to the side of her mouth. "This scene is awfully familiar to me."

"I was in the neighborhood," I said. "Hi, Maddie. It's just me."

Delia said, "Maddie, maybe you should run back to the party. If you hurry you can still watch the fireworks with your friends."

"I don't want to go," she said. "I want to stay here with

you." Then to me, "That looks like my father's watch. He thought Mom threw it away. He's been looking forever."

I hadn't even realized I was still carrying it, but there it was draped across my open hand. I said, "It does? Well, here. You take it to him. If it's not his, maybe he'll let you keep it."

She hesitated a moment, glanced from the watch to Delia and back to the watch, then slipped it gently from my fingers and took off running back toward the party. We watched her until she was in the periphery of the clubhouse light, then Delia said, "Hey," and kissed me on the mouth. She took my hand and pulled me toward the road. I said, "What? Where are we going?"

"We can't stay here," she said. "Sam might come looking."

I let her lead me back into the rough, then across the road toward her house without speaking. There was a high wooden privacy fence around the yard, and she unlatched the side gate, waved me through ahead of her. I shrugged, and she shut the gate. When I reached for her, she ducked my arms and ran around me, her calves bright as ice in the moonlight, headed toward the back of the yard, beyond the range of the porch light. I stood there for a second, watched her disappear into the shadows. I wondered suddenly what Sam Holladay had gotten her for their anniversary. The dress she was wearing or the earrings or the ribbon in her hair. A giant magnolia bush loomed at the rear of the yard and Delia had gone around behind it somewhere. I shut my eyes, then opened them again. I still couldn't see her. I walked in her direction, feeling dizzy and awkward, and when I found her she was sitting in a grassy clearing behind the magnolia with her arms circling her knees.

"Hey," I said. I sat beside her in the grass. "Whatcha doing back here?"

The music from the party sifted through the air, faintly, like it had blended somehow with the darkness. I could almost feel it on my skin. Delia took my hand and played with my fingers, like This Little Piggy. She said, "What's it like to be an orphan? Is that the right word? It sounds so Oliver Twisty. Has that word gone out of fashion—like 'midget'?"

Her voice was matter-of-fact, curious. I didn't think she was being mean.

"I hadn't really thought about it," I said.

"I mean you're completely unattached," she said. "Think about it. You could pick up tomorrow without a care in the world. You could drive to Wisconsin and become a dairy farmer or something and you wouldn't be leaving anything behind."

"Isn't that a movie?" I said.

She said, "You're thinking of the one where the guy goes off and pretends to be Amish to get away from the mob."

"I'd be leaving you behind," I said. "Wouldn't you miss me?"

She tugged at the hem of her dress, smoothed the fabric over her knees. She said, "You know, when Maddie and I were out there on the golf course, I had a feeling you were close. Do you think that's possible? For me to have sensed your presence or something. I'm pretty sure that I knew you were out there."

"Maybe," I said. "I don't know."

I heard a muffled thump in the distance and both of us turned to look. The sky was tracked with red streamers. The fireworks had started without us.

"Yes," she said after a moment. "I'll miss you."

The sky bloomed a second time, three separate bursts, the reports staggering over to us an instant later. I turned to

Delia, but she was watching the show. There had been something I was going to say, but now I couldn't remember what it was. The colored flares played faintly on her forehead and on the bridge of her nose. She looked different somehow than I had imagined she would.

Clairvoyance

A light came on in the kitchen. Delia could see it through the leaves of the magnolia and she knew what it meant—Sam was home, looking for her—but she didn't react right away. The fireworks were still going, one after another now, glittery concussions in the darkling sky. She could feel the pulse in her throat. She edged forward so she could track her husband's progress through the house, watch his shadow playing on the glass. The windows in the living room, then the master bedroom, filled with yellow light. She said, "Sam's here. Or else we're being robbed."

"What? Shit. We'll go over the fence. We can hide at my house."

"No," she said.

Her husband was standing at the bedroom window, one hand holding the curtain back. She watched his eyes scanning the yard, his gaze moving directly over her, registering nothing. She almost stood and waved, as if trying to flag a passing car. The separate halves of her life were bending toward each other at this moment, like convergent time lines in a textbook, and she felt this with a sort of relief. Sam could open the window and say her name and everything would be understood. He could let her go or call her inside, whatever he wanted. If he would only open the window, the weight of making a decision would be lifted from her. Simon touched the back of her wrist and she squeezed his hand. The sky continued to open with light. While she watched, the curtain fell shut, the window went dark, the night closed over them like a shroud.

It was then that Delia realized she was trembling. Simon put his arms around her and pulled her against him and said, "It's all right. He's gone. No need to be afraid." She let him hold her, pressed her brow against his throat. Her hands felt heavy, her shoulders weak. Beneath the fireworks and the rustle of his clothes, she could hear crickets whispering in the grass.

"My mother used to jump out of closets to scare us." His lips moved against her hair. "Me and my dad. She liked being afraid, said it cut through all the crap, though I don't think she ever used that actual word. 'Crap,' I mean."

She pulled away, one hand still touching his chest.

"That's a strange thing to say right now."

He dropped his eyes, shrugged. The light glancing through the leaves made him look young, his skin smooth, his lashes delicate. In his face, she could see the image of every boy she had ever known—all the desperate hands and reckless kisses and urgent loving—and she adored him for the memory. She let her fingers run along his neck, his cheekbone, the line of his jaw. She took his hand and kissed his knuckles.

"I'm sorry," she said. "It was a fine thing to say."

"I guess it was out of the blue."

"No, she was right. Your mother knew what she was talking about."

Delia stood and brushed the back of her dress. She could hear a dog barking down the street, manic over the fireworks. An airplane passed overhead and she looked at the sky until she found the wing lights, imagined the passengers, some of them reading the paper, some of them asleep, oblivious to the bedlam on the planet down below. Simon reached over and circled her ankle with his thumb and forefinger and she said, "I need to get back. Sam'll be worried."

He nodded but didn't let her go.

"We'll talk tomorrow," she said. "When we get back from church, Sam always goes out for breakfast supplies. He loves a big Sunday breakfast. I'll call when he's gone. Okay?"

"All right then," he said. "Tomorrow."

He released her ankle, and she moved back a few steps, then opened and closed her hand and turned away, trying not to hurry across the yard. The night felt humid, quiet behind the fireworks, the way it felt before a rain. Her footsteps sounded lonely on the empty street. She found Sam in a wrought iron chair on the country club patio watching the pyrotechnics with a drink. He started when she appeared, but she put a hand on his shoulder to keep him in his seat. Before he could ask where she had been, she told him she was just out walking on the golf course—it was peaceful there and she wanted to be alone for a while. Apparently, Maddie hadn't mentioned why she left.

Sam said, "Is everything all right? I saw the little girl come back."

"Everything's fine," she said. "Is she here?"

Sam pointed and she could see Maddie on the grass beside her father, her eyes on the grand finale, her mouth slack with amazement and delight. She was still young enough to be dazzled by fireworks. At that moment, the choice that she would have to make came back to Delia. She couldn't for all the world see a way to love them both. What she wanted, more than anything, was a way to plot the courses of their lives, like navigating by the stars, a way to see into two separate futures. When she was a girl, she would ask her mother what she thought had become of her father. Her mother would stop whatever she was doing and cover her eyes and a ghostly sound would escape her lips as though she were slipping into a sort of psychic trance. I see a man, she would say, a man drunk and in prison, a thief and a killer and a womanizer. True or not, imagining that her father was a heartless man was a way to understand what he had done. That's what Delia wanted. Second sight, the gift of clairvoyance. She wanted to understand what was going to happen to them.

She told Sam she was ready to leave, and he didn't protest. On their way back, the rain started up, fat summery drops, and Sam took off his jacket and held it over their heads while they ran, shoulders bumping, to the door. He kissed her in the foyer, and she could feel the warmth of his skin through the fabric of his shirt. He led her down the hall to the bedroom, stopping to push out of his shoes. She didn't see how she could refuse him this. She didn't want to refuse him. He was her husband. They made love with the kindness of an ending, though Delia could not have said for certain that it was. Their wet clothes were strewn across the carpet. For the first time in a long time, she tasted the salt on his neck, smelled the musty and familiar way he smelled, felt the gentle consideration in his hands. When they were finished, she lay with her head on his chest and listened to his heart beat until it began to slow, falling off into the steady rhythm of sleep.

"Are you awake?" she said.

"No," he said after a moment, "I'm sleeping, dead to the world. I'm dreaming of you right this minute."

"What do you see?"

"Wait," he said. She traced her fingers through the hair on his chest, ran her instep along his calf. He said, "Yes, here it is. You're riding naked down the beach on a white stallion, wearing a headdress made entirely of ostrich feathers. You look very important."

She yanked a hair on his chest, and he groaned, clapped a hand over hers. She rolled away from him, her head still resting on his outstretched arm. She said, "I was hoping you might be dreaming of my future."

"I was," he said, and she kicked him under the covers with her heel. Through the window, she could see the magnolia bush, the rain pattering on the leaves. She thought of her husband standing in this very room, looking at her beyond the glass and not seeing anything. The half-circle of porch light stopped just short of where she'd been. Gradually, his breathing slowed, grew more shallow until she knew he was asleep. She waited a moment, then sat up and looked at him, the lines in his face relaxed, his lips parted just slightly, the covers bunched at his fleshy middle, his skin mottled and wan. He was as vulnerable as a child, completely open to her. She wondered what she could possibly have done to deserve that sort of trust.

She climbed out of bed, careful not to disturb her husband, and walked over to the window. The light was soft and supple on her bare skin. She was tired of the summer, she thought. The heat and the insects and the rain. The way the air itself seemed to clamor for attention. She looked forward to the smoky haze of fall, the quiet of winter. Just then, something caught her attention, a shape, a glimmer of motion in the yard. And there was Simon Bell coming out from behind the magnolia bush, blinking, drenched, looking up into the sky with squinted eyes. She thought he had been there all along. His pants were plastered to his legs, his shirt so wet she could see his skin. He shook the water from his hands, like it was possible to get dry in the middle of a storm.

She draped an arm across her breasts, covering herself, then realized the foolishness of her modesty and let it fall again. He must have seen her moving, because right at that moment, he looked in her direction and smiled and gave her a ridiculous wave. She wanted to laugh. Her heart felt huge and cramped behind her ribs. While she watched, he tilted his head and his features went soft, his gaze traveling the length of her, his eyes mesmerized, polished-looking in the rainy light, his face composed and serene, as though he were watching a daydream unfold on her body.

She felt the blood coming to her skin, a sudden conscious ache in her lungs that made it difficult to breathe. She stepped away from the window and pressed her back against the wall. The air conditioner raised goose bumps on her stomach and shoulders. Her husband was snoring quietly in the bed. Nothing had happened yet and she wanted to preserve the moment, because in it she could still love them both. She covered her eyes with her hands, the way her mother had, and tried to imagine the future. With surprising clarity, she saw herself pulling on a robe and walking out into the rain and leading Simon home. He would get them each a bottle of beer, and she'd tell him that she wished there was a way to make things different, to take it all back, but she knew it was impossible. So she would tell him the truth. He was the one she was going to have to hurt. They would be sitting on the couch, pool light waving on the walls and skimming around on his face, and he'd ask her if she loved him, and she would be unable to tell him no. But her feelings for him didn't change anything. She had made promises to her husband, and she didn't love him any less despite what she had done. While they talked, the rain would stop. The beer would feel sour and warm in her stomach. Simon would turn on the television with the remote and watch for a moment, a commercial for a used car lot—she saw it all that clearly—then turn it off. He would put his hands on her face and kiss her and she would let him. She would give him one kiss full of everything that was in her heart, her sadness at losing him, her resolve that this was the only possible way to make things right. When they were finished, she would say good-bye and sneak back to her husband's house and slip into bed beside him and listen to him breathing in the darkness for a long time.

And so something very much like what she imagined did in fact come to pass. The details might have been a little different, the way the pool lights played upon the walls or the taste of the beer, the exact nature of the television commercial or the tenor of Simon's voice when he told her good-bye, but the results of her decision were, in the end, more or less the same.

Part 4

And you my loves, few as there have been, let's lie and say it could never have been otherwise.

So that: we may glide off in peace, not howling like orphans in this endless century of war.

—Jim Harrison

Pool Lights

It was in the summer that I made love to my next-door neighbor's wife. She led me by the hand back to her husband's bed and unbuttoned my shirt, slipping it over my shoulders, her lips on my neck and chest. I was wearing a pair of her husband's shorts that were way too big, and she pulled them over my narrow hips without having to undo the buttons or the zipper. Both of us thought that was funny and laughed between kisses.

It was summer when I watched her dive from the platform of my father's pool. Her husband was out of town at some sort of history conference, and it was late enough that we figured the neighbors were asleep. She drifted underwater toward where I was standing in the shallow end and came up blinking and smoothing her hair back on her head, the pool lights giving her a strange, almost magical sheen. We stood there for a long time just looking at each other, not touching, my nostrils stinging from chlorine. A light came on over at Bob Robinson's house—Bob was always a light sleeper—and we ducked down beneath the rim of the pool and stayed hidden until it went off again. While we waited, my heart knocking against my ribs, I had this crazy idea that if we could just stay where we where, submerged to our chins, Delia spitting pool water from her mouth, shivering a little, her hand finding the waistband of my shorts beneath the water, then everything would be preserved, that perilous moment and the air and Delia's goose-bumped shoulder beneath my hand.

But we didn't stay in the pool, of course. Her toes and fingertips wrinkled, and we danced across the flagstone patio and into the house and piled into the shower together. I sat on the edge of the tub and washed her hair. She told me a story about an ice storm in Mississippi of all places. She was hunched forward, her eyes closed against the suds, her belly folding prettily. I thought, just then, that I could imagine her as a girl, going to clean houses with her mother, watching her father play piano at the Ramada Inn on Saturday nights. She still had a knot on her collarbone where she'd broken it pretending to be a gymnast in her backyard and a faint scar across the bridge of her nose from trying to ride a unicycle and crashing into the curb. I told her that I wished I had known her then, instead of now, and she laughed and told me I was crazy.

A few weeks before I moved back into my parents' house, this friend of mine, Lamont Turner, became separated from his wife. While he was at work one day, his wife went over to the house and took their dog. Portnoy belonged to both of them, technically, but Lamont was lunatic with despair when the dog turned up missing and enlisted me in a plan to get him back. My job was simple, just go over to the house where Ellen was staying and keep her busy while he crept around the back and swiped the dog. I did as he asked, went over there and talked to her, and it wasn't long before the conversation turned to why she left in the first place. She said that what she wanted from Lamont was a leap of faith—her exact words—that they'd grown comfortable and complacent, and he wasn't trying very hard to love her anymore. At that moment, as if on cue, Lamont appeared at the top of the high wooden privacy fence that surrounded the backyard. He was wearing some kind of ninja suit, baggy black pants and gloves and a sweatshirt with a hood. He dropped to the grass in a Kung Fu crouch, scurried across the yard, slung old Portnoy over his shoulder—he'd been dozing comfortably on the patio and didn't seem all that surprised to see his master dressed in black, running a sub-rosa rescue mission—and hurried back to the fence. I tried to keep myself from laughing, but he was the most ridiculous and pitiful thing I'd ever seen. Ellen, she turned to look where I was looking just when Lamont was cresting the fence a second time. As they were going over the top, Lamont glanced back in our direction, and at that exact moment, the fence gave way beneath him, the crossbars buckling, vertical planks splintering, sending him face first into the pavement. By the time we got out there, he'd managed to roll over on his back, one hand dangling limp and broken from his wrist, his face a mess of blood and tissue, a piece of shin-bone tenting the fabric of his pants. Portnoy was bounding around, licking everybody, probably the most alive he'd been in years. Before he passed out, Lamont croaked, "Ellen?" Though I don't think that was exactly what his wife had in mind when she asked for a leap of faith, the two of them had been together ever since.

Delia howled when I told her this story. It was the day before my birthday and we were sitting in the living room of my parents' house, watching the pool lights flicker on the walls. I wasn't sure why I'd told the story—maybe just to see her laugh—but suddenly, watching her rock back on the couch, it seemed like a sad and lovely thing Lamont had done. It was the only real love story that I knew to tell. I thought about my parents, how they'd stayed together for years after my mother's affair. How they went on watching horror movies, my father drawing her against him because he knew her fear was real. When she was young, my mother had wanted to be an actress, but she didn't aspire to serious roles—charwomen and battered wives. She wanted space-ships on her lawn or maniacs in the closet. She wanted to be King Kong's girlfriend. I wondered if that's why she'd done it, for the heat of the thing, the madhouse rush, if that's why she had betrayed my father. I didn't blame her really. My father was not an easy man to live with. I knew that. And I understood how hard it must have been, as well, to live with what she'd done.

At that moment, listening to Delia laugh in the darkness, I started hearing this strange far-off wind sound in my head, and I felt a pressure in my stomach, like I'd been punched, like I had swallowed a pool's worth of water. I couldn't breathe right, and my pulse was jumpy, and I turned away and counted to myself until I'd settled down. Delia wanted to know what was wrong, and I told her nothing. Everything was fine. Everything would always be fine.

It was still summer when she ended things between us. I had, as usual, forgotten to turn the pool lights off, and the walls were green with the reflection. Delia was wearing this white cotton robe that made her shoulders perfect and gathered light to her. She said she wasn't going to tell Sam about us. She believed that things could go back to the way they were before. I promised her that I wouldn't try to change her mind. It was as if we were acting out a scene from a movie, some English film where all the characters are very modern and polite and everyone understood why people did the things they do. When she was gone, I sat there a while trying to find some sadness in me. But I was blank, like none of this was real, and I would wake up in the morning, wait for Sam Holladay to leave the house, then steal over to the golf course and find Delia there, and we'd begin all over again.

When I did wake, it was still dark outside and cold in the house from the air-conditioning, and the windows were drenched in condensation. The clock by the bed showed 4:57 A.M. I rolled over and picked up the phone and started to dial Delia's number before I remembered what had happened. The numbers on the phone were glowing an eerie, fluorescent green. I didn't feel anything yet, though I knew that it would come. I hung up and pulled on a bathrobe, fixed a glass of beer in the kitchen, and went outside.

The rain had come drifting back, the finest of mists. It muffled sound, giving the street a pleasant silence. I remembered that it was Sunday. My neighbors would be pulling themselves together in a few hours and going to church like good people.

Across the street, the golf course was empty, the tall pines shimmering with moisture. I thought about Betty Fowler down the road, the rain drowning out the quiet in her house. I pictured her in the high-backed chair in her living room, her lips working awkwardly around one of her favorite curse words, and I couldn't help laughing a little. She was always asking me if I was in love, and I'd think, no, that can't be right, you don't allow yourself to fall in love with someone else's wife. I could almost see her then, curving in sleep toward her husband's side of the bed. She was alone in the world. I wondered if it was true that her husband had buried a chest of gold coins in the fairway across the street or, even more unlikely, that she could find those coins with her divining rod.

I tried to imagine divining in scientific terms. Tiny particles of intent, passing invisibly, delicately, from the rod into its bearer, leading him toward his intended destination. It was as unbelievable as light. Facts were supposed to be easy. I was standing barefoot on the damp, polished asphalt. The road was beaded with rainwater, the street lights catching in puddles. I was alone. Those were facts, real and incontrovertible.

I'd heard of faith healers and their patients who could believe away illness. There was a newspaper article about a woman so riddled with cancer that she couldn't lift herself from bed, couldn't bring a cup of soup to her lips. This was in Texas. A preacher came to her and promised that he could heal her through prayer, and he did it, or both of them did, not just convinced themselves that the cancer was gone but believed it into actual medical remission. The papers called it a bona fide miracle. I was thinking maybe Betty Fowler's belief, more than anything else, might lead her to the gold. Or maybe there was something in all of us, some built-in radar or biological lodestone, that was leading us always toward a predetermined place in time.

I used to believe in things. When my parents went to church—my father tagged along reluctantly for the first few years of their marriage, then stopped going altogether—they would deposit me, along with the other young children, in a Sunday School class. We would spend the morning learning the mysteries of religion from hooded nuns. They taught us the Trinity and the virgin birth and the Ascension and even such minor miracles as the stigmata. They taught us of St.

Francis of Assisi and Anna Emmerich and the Belgian girl, Louise Lateau, all supernaturally marked with the wounds of Christ on their hands and feet, the slash of a sword in their side, even the faint, bloody impression left by the crown of thorns. I believed it, then, or at least was willing to entertain the possibility.

And there was Atlantis, when I was a kid, the magnificent undersea city, light-years ahead of the land bound in technology. I dreamed of finding it on a pleasure dive and stumbling into fame and fortune and a beautiful water-breathing woman who longed to see the stars and sun and moon.

There was, as well, the TV magician who levitated the beautiful woman in a shining evening gown—there was always a beautiful woman—and when he passed the hoops around her, no strings attached, part of me was trying to figure out how he did it and the other part believed, marveled in the realization that he *was* doing it. Here was the woman, face turned toward the camera, eyes wide in surprise, and there was the hoop passing the length of her, head to high-heeled shoes, and there were no strings and she was flying. It was a joy to watch her fly.

The last night that Delia stayed at my house, I woke near midnight and found her missing. Blue moonlight was streaming through the windows. The air was full of familiar sounds. She was gone. I couldn't feel her warmth on the mattress or trace the subtle depression of the place she had lain. I thought maybe she'd never really been there at all. I had conjured her into a dream so real as to be barely distinguishable from the truth, one of those dreams that you wake from believing. But at my house, it was still night and the air was humming with summer music, insects and airplanes and cars on the road. I said her name, and she didn't answer. I went to the window and saw the pool glimmering with light and the next row of houses beyond my fence, lumps of deeper darkness against the sky. Right then, I spotted Delia sitting cross-legged on the grass, wearing my white t-shirt. The shirt was so full of odd moonlight it might have been electric. She stood and walked a few steps, not knowing I was watching her, into a circle of darkness on the far side of the pool. She was gone again, an illusion. She was invisible to me, and I was frightened breathless.

Now, I could make out a light in one of the windows of Bob Robinson's house. It made me feel a little better to know someone else was sleepless at this hour. One of the children probably had a nightmare and needed to be comforted. I was thinking about how no one ever called my number—in case of emergency, Bob had said—and how I should have been glad about that, but sitting here in the dark, the rain so fine it was like walking through spiderwebs, I wasn't glad at all.

I watched the light in the window for passing shadows, signs of life, but didn't see anything. After a while, I realized that there wasn't a light inside, just a reflection from the streetlamp on the wet glass. They were all sleeping soundly. I was alone. I got to my feet and marched across the road to the golf course, the fairway soaked through, rainwater pushing up between my toes. I could feel myself moving toward something, but I didn't know what. The rough was mostly young, sappy pines, pliable and elastic, but I managed to break a limb loose. It was forked with a long shaft, the sort Mrs. Fowler had described. I stood in the middle of the sixteenth fairway with my eyes closed and tried to focus, tried to feel something. How had Mrs. Fowler described it? The memory of a magnetic attraction, a dream of electricity. Walking felt right, just then, so I headed off down the strip of grass, my eyes still shut tight, but I couldn't feel anything. Mrs. Fowler would have said that I didn't know what I was looking for. And she would have been right, if she'd been there to say it. I didn't have the slightest idea.

The grass was slick beneath my feet. I opened my mouth to catch rain on my tongue, eyes still closed, still moving forward, when suddenly I was falling. The ground disappeared, and there was this moment, before I went plunging into the water hazard, when I opened my eyes and I could see my house across the street, lights going in the bedroom and the kitchen, and I could see Delia's face in my mind as clearly as if she was standing there before me. I remembered sitting in her backyard just a few hours before, the rain drumming on my shoulders, and finding myself unable to leave, as though if I moved from that spot, I might break some marvelous enchantment, some spell that Delia and I had spent the summer casting, all full of blindness and passion and whatever else is necessary to make two people give up a part of themselves. Then I went rolling down the embankment and into the water, sputtering and flopping around like a maniac. It was only a few feet deep, but I kept losing my balance and going ass-backward into the muck. By the time I got myself together, I was drenched, my feet stockinged with mud, my bathrobe heavy as a hundred stones.

As I was making my way back to the road, I heard Bob Robinson's voice.

"What the hell's going on out here? Is that you, Bell, you cocksucker? What in God's name are you doing? Scared me shitless."

He was leaning against the split rail fence, wearing a red nightshirt that reached to his knees, his belly pressing against the fabric. I wiped the mud out of my eyes. He said, "God-dam, look at you. I came out here for a smoke, and it sounded like a circus animal had gotten loose on the golf course."

"I fell in the water hazard," I said. "I didn't know you smoked."

He nodded. "Quit for fifteen years. But I'm back now and better than ever. I figured my lungs had enough of a vacation. The wife won't let me smoke in the house."

We stood there for a minute not talking. Bob smoked in the darkness. After a while, he said, "Can I ask what you were doing out there?"

"I'd rather you didn't," I said.

"All I need to hear." He held his hands up and leaned back away from me. Took a drag of his cigarette. "You all right? Anything you want to talk about?"

"I'm okay," I said. Then, "Listen, I thought I saw a light on in your house a minute ago. How long've you been up?"

"Just now," he said. "I woke up in the middle of the night wanting a cigarette a couple of days ago and it's been that way since. Dead asleep, then wham! Gotta have a smoke. People are funny, myself included."

The rain was almost gone, just a faint, ghostly presence, as if the air itself were damp. Not even enough to bother the ember on Bob's cigarette. I stepped through the fence so I was on his side and scraped the bottom of my feet in the road, trying to clean a little mud.

I said, "You remember when you first moved to town and you wanted to list me as an emergency number for the school?"

"Sure. The wife made you an angel food cake," he said.

"Devil's food," I said. "Would you have wanted them to call me? If something had happened. I mean, thank God nothing did, but if it had? You would have trusted me with your kids?"

"You bet," he said. "Abso-fucking-lutely."

"Thanks," I said.

I wanted to tell him everything just then, me and Delia and my parents. I wanted to sit him down and spin my life story in the darkness just to see what he thought. Bob was bound to have an opinion. He had an opinion on everything. I wanted to tell him what I decided in that moment when I was falling, when I was still between the ground and the water and I could see the lights of my parents' house. I wanted to tell him that I couldn't be alone anymore. But I didn't. I waited with him until he'd finished his cigarette, then we said good night, and he thanked me for finding his watch, showed it to me on his wrist, and we made our separate ways home.

Inside, I put on a pot of coffee and drank a second beer, then another, while I waited for the coffee to brew. I knew I wouldn't be able to go back to sleep. I stood in the kitchen and watched the backyard through the window over the sink, the pool dimpled with mist. There was a phone on the wall in the kitchen. I grabbed the dangling cord and jerked the phone off the hook and dialed the number in my head. It rang for a long time, ten, fifteen rings, and when Delia answered I hung up with my thumb. I waited a moment, got myself together and called back. This time she answered on the first ring.

"Sorry," I said. "That was me that hung up before."

She said, "I thought so. You can't be calling here, Simon. Sam'll wake up."

I didn't say anything for a minute. I could hear her breathing.

"What do you want, Simon?"

"You," I said. "I want us to be together."

She said, "I don't think that's a good idea."

I stretched out flat on my back, water seeping out of my robe and my hair onto the floor. Like blood, I thought. I imagined myself the victim of a hideous crime. Police officers chalking my outline on the linoleum. There was a long silence between us when I thought she might hang up. I said, "Did I ever tell you that my mother committed suicide?"

"No," she said, quietly. "You told me that she drowned."

"She did," I said. "She just walked into the water. I was thinking about what you said. About that river in Mississippi. It reminded me of her."

"That was just a story. Something that happened to me. I'm sorry, Simon," she said. "I have to go. I am sorry."

I laid the phone on my chest and crossed my hands over it, then straightened my legs so I was positioned like a corpse. I closed my eyes. I pictured myself leaping off of a high cliff. I could see myself falling, growing smaller, distant, as if I were filming the fall, see a puff of dust rise when I hit the ground. A funny thud, like the coyote in cartoons. The computer phone operator was saying that if I would like to make a call I should hang up and try again. I did what she wanted.

"Hey," I said, when Delia answered.

"Stop calling, please, Simon," she said. "Even Sam can't sleep through this many phone calls. We'll talk more in a couple of days. Okay?"

I said, "I just thought I'd see what you were doing."

"I'm not doing anything," she said. "You woke me up before, and I can't go back to sleep. Are you okay?"

"I'm sorry I woke you," I said.

I heard her turn on a light. I thought of her arms, long and slender, faintly muscled. Nice. This whole thing was nice. Her soft voice. The cold, the dark, the rain. She and I.

"Where are you?" I said.

"In the living room," she said. "I'm watching television. Are you okay?"

"Yes, I'm fine," I said. "I'm thinking about making a leap of faith."

"What exactly do you mean by that?" Her voice sounded concerned and that made me feel better. "You're not going to hurt yourself, are you?"

"Don't be silly," I said. "I'm fine."

She said, "After the talk about suicide and then leaping, I thought maybe, you know."

"No, this is a good thing, I think."

"Are you really okay, Simon?" she said.

"I'm okay, really," I said and hung up softly. Dawn light was creeping over the ceiling, mixing in with the glimmer of the pool. Fingers of shadow on the walls. The bitter smell of burned coffee. I was soaking wet, but I wasn't really cold. After a moment, I called back and when she answered, I said, "I forgot to tell you good night."

"You're sweet," she said. It sounded like she was crying. "Good night. I'm taking the phone off the hook."

That quick, she was gone. I could feel a part of myself, a distant, better part, attaching itself to her voice and traveling toward her through the wires. I knew that I should do what she wanted, let her go back to her life with Sam Holladay, let the days widen the space between us—all my life, I had been putting distance between myself and the world—but knowing this didn't stop me from loving Delia. Whatever was good in me belonged to her now. No matter what we had done, no matter the messy circumstances of our lives. I would not let her drift quietly away. Without her, without the part of me that she brought to life, like a trick of ancient and wonderful magic, I might as well have closed my eyes and let myself fade into the long, indifferent sleep of the dead.

The Girl in the Sundress

At church that morning, Sam Holladay sat behind a young woman in a flowered sundress. She was about sixteen, lovely, there alone as far as Holladay could tell. Sunlight filtered through the stained glass and played in blues and reds on her bare arms. He kept thinking that she reminded him of someone, the reddish hair and pale skin, the way her shoulders moved beneath her dress. And then it came to him: Mary Youngblood. He couldn't believe he hadn't seen it sooner, the same delicate features, the same tilt of the head as though she was listening carefully to something that he couldn't hear. During the homily, he watched her shoulders start to shake, like she was crying, then her hand dip into her purse and come out with a tissue. She dabbed her eyes and kept listening and sobbed quietly. He wanted to touch her, to be certain that she was real. He nudged Delia and nodded in the girl's direction, and Delia made a sympathetic face as if to acknowledge how awful it was that such a pretty girl could be so full of sorrow. He asked Delia what the sermon had been about, as they were turning onto Speaking Pines

Road—he had already forgotten—thinking perhaps that the words were what made the girl cry, but she couldn't remember either.

It was at that moment when he saw Simon Bell sitting in his yard. As he swung the car into the driveway, Simon stood and hurried in their direction, and Holladay had the distinct impression—he could not have explained it in a million years—that something important was about to happen and that it had something to do with the girl in church. Maybe it was the way Simon looked, his hair a tangle of curls, his face stubbled and dirty, his eyes red-rimmed and delirious and as wretched as the girl in the sundress. Or maybe it was the just the way he often felt after church, a little sleepy and disoriented but rejuvenated at the same time, convinced that what people did mattered in the world. Regardless, Simon came over to the car and pressed his hands against the window on Delia's side, and Holladay couldn't quit thinking about the girl.

Delia said, "Shit, shit. Sam, go inside. Shit."

"What?" he said. "What's going on?"

Simon tried the handle on Delia's side, but it was locked. He was saying something, and at first, Holladay couldn't understand what it was. Then he got it, more from the motion of Simon's lips than anything else. Holladay said, "Is he telling you that he loves you?"

"Shit, Sam," Delia said. "Oh, fuck. Let me out. Simon," she was yelling now, "go back to your house. I'll come talk to you in a minute. Get out of here. Go home, please. Please. Sam, let me out."

Holladay got out of the car and Delia slipped out behind him just as Simon Bell was rounding the trunk of the car. Holladay stepped forward and grabbed his shoulders, still feeling strangely apart from what was happening, still convinced that somehow all of this was connected to the girl in church.

"I'm sorry, but I love her, Sam," he said. "And she loves me. Don't you, Delia? Tell him that you're in love with me."

He struggled, but not much, and Holladay was able to hold him still. Over his shoulder, Holladay said, "Delia, go inside. Let me and Simon talk for a minute."

He was surprised at how calm he was, given what he was to understand from Simon's words. His wife was sleeping with another man, his darkest suspicions confirmed. His life, as he had understood it up to that moment, was rearranging itself before his eyes. But he kept seeing the girl in the sundress, kept trying to decipher how she figured into what was happening.

"Christ, Sam," Delia said. "I'm not—"

"Go inside," he said again and something in his voice made her do as he asked. He watched her walk backward halfway to the door, then turn away and jog up the steps and into the house, Simon calling after her to wait, wait, wait, but she was already gone. Holladay led Simon back into his own yard, one arm across his shoulders, like the two of them were old friends. They stood there a minute watching the door, as if both of them expected Delia to come bursting back out into the morning at any minute.

Holladay said, "She's beautiful, isn't she?"

"Yes," Simon said. Then, after a moment, "I love her, Sam."

"So you said."

Across the street, Betty Fowler was standing on the sixteenth fairway with her divining rod. She looked shadowy, a silhouette in the new light. Holladay couldn't tell whether or not she was watching them, but he didn't care.

Simon said, "I want to be with her."

"Do you ever go to church?" Holladay said.

"No," he said, sounding surprised.

Holladay nodded, thoughtfully, and said, "We just came from there. I think I fell in love today."

"This is not the reaction I expected."

"Yes," he said, blinking. "I don't know. There was a girl in the pew in front of us in a flowered dress. Maybe she was sixteen years old. Beautiful. She was sitting a little to one side, so I could see her profile. She reminded me of someone I knew a long time ago."

He was looking at Simon Bell, studying his face and the mud caked on his robe. He thought that this man believed what he said about Delia. He knew the sort of fear he could see in Simon Bell's eyes, and it came from the idea of losing her. He said, "This girl. She had a gorgeous neck. Slim and tan. Long with wisps of red hair falling on it from her ponytail. She was crying. We didn't know why. I swear to you, just looking at her neck and the curve of muscle in her shoulder, I fell in love with her. For the whole hour. You think that's possible?"

"If she was only sixteen, I think an hour is plenty long for you to be in love with her," he said and Holladay laughed.

"No, you don't understand," he said. "She wasn't Delia. When we were walking out, I held the door for her—God, I felt like such a kid—and as she was passing, it hit me. She wasn't Delia. Delia wasn't this vision in a flowered dress in church. And all the feeling just went away."

"So what are you saying? Are you telling me that you love her more? Is that what you're saying to me?"

"No," Holladay said. "Only that I love her, too."

"Well," Simon said, quiet and embarrassed. He covered

his forehead with his hand and sighed, then let the hand fall limply against his leg. He looked bewildered, his eyes watery, his mouth open. He said, "I thought I knew something. I'd made up my mind." He looked toward the door, then back at Holladay. "I don't have the slightest idea what to do next. I'm sorry, Sam."

Holladay nodded again, as if that were the most reasonable thing in the world for him to say. He was thinking that none of them would ever be happy again and then he said it, just like that. "None of us will ever be happy again."

"That isn't true," Simon said. "It's not true."

Holladay said, "Wait here. I'll be right back. I just want to get something from the house. I'll come back, and we'll straighten this thing out, all right?"

Simon started to say something, then stopped and shrugged like he understood what was about to happen and had resigned himself to it. Sam Holladay did know what was going to happen. It was perfectly clear to him. He went inside and found Delia in the kitchen and smiled at her across the cooking island. She said she was sorry and she didn't mean for him to find out this way. Before she could say anything else, he told her it didn't matter. He understood. He was old, and she was young, and he really did believe that she still loved him, despite everything. He paid attention to the way her hair was swinging at her cheeks, the way she touched her lips with her fingers. He wanted to memorize every detail, because he was sure, even then, that his life with her was over and that the time was past for a new beginning. He clicked on the radio, knowing that she would turn the volume up, and asked her if she wouldn't mind cooking breakfast now. He was hungry, he said. He waited until she began taking the copper pots from their hangers over the stove, then went back to the bedroom and took the gun from beneath the mattress. Morning light was slanting through the blinds making everything look dreamy and weightless. He remembered Delia in the dress he'd gotten her for their anniversary, that awful last-minute dress, blue with white sailboats and a white belt. The sort of dress a woman his age might wear. She was putting on an earring in the bedroom doorway, preparing for their celebration, assuring him that the dress was fine, lovely, just what she'd been wanting. And she did make it look beautiful somehow. He wondered if this wasn't exactly what was supposed to happen. That was the way of things. Just when you least expected it to, the world made awful and perfect sense. Of all of them, he thought, Delia would find love again. Someone was always loving Delia. He flipped open the chamber, checked to make sure the gun was loaded, then slipped out the door, letting it close quietly behind him.

Greyhounds

When the dispatch came, Sheriff Lawrence Nightingale was standing with his fingers hooked into a ten-foot chain link fence, looking for his dog. Nightingale had adopted a greyhound. A month before, he had taken his deputies down to Mobile for a sensitivity training course—just because Sherwood was a sleepy county didn't mean the department should fall behind the times—and they had gone out to the track as a reward for sitting through the dry, mostly ridiculous lectures. Taped to every betting window were signs that said, FOR JUST $2.00 A MONTH, YOU CAN HELP AN OLD RACING DOG RETIRE LIKE A CHAMP. Below the words were two cartoon greyhounds, the first wire thin, desperate and hungry, sniffing around a sinister-looking Dumpster, and the other, broad-chested and healthy, standing in a field of clover, surrounded by his trophies.

Nightingale had thought it was probably a scam. Somebody was taking the money and putting the dogs to sleep. But he did a little investigating and discovered an actual farm, less than an hour from town, where the greyhounds could live as long as they found a benefactor. He even got a photo of his dog, just like in those television commercials for Third World children. His dog's racing name had been Joaquim's White Heat, but Nightingale called him Bill, after his own dead father.

Most mornings, before he went on duty, he drove out to watch the greyhounds run. The place looked like a sort of heaven to Nightingale, thirty or so dogs waiting to be turned out for their first good exercise of the day—whining, rattling their kennel gates, then breaking into the field at full, gorgeous speed, ears pinned back like arrowheads. Tired dogs snaking through the grass on their bellies, scrapping happily, growling over nothing, then dashing off again, because running was what they understood.

He could see Bill galloping with the other dogs, his ribcage pulsing, his coat bluish in the morning light. He clicked his tongue and called his name as the pack passed, their steps the muted sound of drumming fingers, but Bill kept racing. He didn't think the dog knew his new name yet, but Nightingale couldn't bring himself to use the old one. Too showy. Most days, it made him feel good to come out here, the simple bliss of speed infecting him, but this morning had been ruined by the radio dispatch. The dogs looked like phantoms. He got into his car, swung a U-turn on the highway, and sped toward town.

For Sam Holladay's sake, he didn't run the siren.

Nightingale had known the man a long time, had been a student in his history class seventeen years before. When he arrived at the house, emergency personnel were milling around in the yard, an ambulance and two patrol cars parked along the curb. Sam Holladay was sitting in the grass about ten yards from the body, wearing a tie and suspenders, no jacket. He had his knees drawn up, his eyes focused on the horizon above the golf course. Nightingale made certain that someone was keeping an eye on the wife, then walked over, touched two fingers to Bell's neck and felt nothing. His skin was already growing cold, rubbery.

"Shit, Mr. Holladay," he said.

Nightingale rubbed his fingertips together, trying to shake the chill left by the dead man's skin. He wiped them on his pants, held them against his lips and blew warm air across his nails. He didn't look at the body.

"What happened?"

Holladay didn't answer. Nightingale felt strange. He'd seen dead bodies before but not enough, he guessed, to have grown accustomed to the sight. He was slow and slightly nauseous, like the one and only time he'd gotten stoned in the army. He could feel the sun on his forearms but was chilled all the same. Nightingale looked at Sam Holladay, his chin tilted upward, the skin at his neck loose. He was an old man, not a killer.

He said, "I've gotta arrest you, Mr. Holladay. If you don't tell me what happened, I'll ask your wife."

"No sense in that. He's dead. I killed him," he said. "You can call me Sam if you want. You're old enough now."

"Shit, Mr. Holladay," he said again.

He called a deputy over to take Sam Holladay to the station. At the time, it seemed like the proper thing to question Mrs. Holladay himself. He stood with the old man until the car arrived, instructed the deputy to let Mr. Holladay ride in the front seat, if that's what he wanted, then made the rounds of the neighbors, Betty Fowler and Bob Robinson, who was at work, putting off for as long as he could the grim and painful trip up the driveway to ask this woman what reason her husband might have to ruin all these lives.

Nightingale was beguiled by crime. He had boxes of mob movies and old newsreels of famous criminals, and he'd slip a tape into the VCR when he was going to bed with the idea that the background noise—all the gunshots and tough talk and high speed chases—might influence his dreams. He conjured visions of bank jobs and gang violence and hostage situations, the way a child called pleasant thoughts to mind to ward away nightmares. Nothing like the movies ever happened in Sherwood, but he wanted to be able to handle himself properly when and if the time ever came.

Now something had happened and Nightingale was botching the job. Simon Bell was dead and Sam Holladay was in jail and Nightingale had been too nervous to question Delia. He'd gone over, as planned, found her sitting in her living room with a deputy. She had an almost empty drink in her hand. When she looked up at him, her eyes flat and lovely as water, her lips parted at the rim of the glass, he said, "Hey," his voice going high, his legs twitchy. He told himself that he'd been around too long to be shaken by the sight of a beautiful woman, but the evidence, in this case, was clear.

When he returned the next day, she was drunk. She led him to the back of the house, the bedroom, where she'd been going though an old steamer trunk, the floor littered with papers and old photographs. She was wearing a white robe, blemished here and there with recent-looking stains, and when she crossed her legs, Indian-style, her thighs came exposed, the trim of cream-colored panties just visible at the fold. He looked at her feet.

"You all right?" he said.

"I'm drunk," she said, pointing at a glass on the floor. The ice had all melted, the liquor looked diluted. "I couldn't think of anything else to do."

"You should get some sleep."

"This is Sam in college," she said, holding up a black and white of three men in old-fashioned suits. "He's in the middle. I'd never seen this picture before last night. He was a funny-looking kid. Look at those ears."

"I need to ask you a few questions," he said.

She didn't answer. Nightingale stood and put his hands in his pockets, came out with a silver dollar and rolled it absently over his knuckles. He walked over to the window and looked out at the yard.

"Is that a silver dollar?" Delia said. "You don't see those much anymore."

"Oh," he said, realizing what was in his hand for the first time. It must have been the coin the old lady had made disappear. He wondered how she'd managed to get it into his pocket without him noticing, then remembered what she'd told him about two people being in love. He said, "I need to ask you if you have any idea why Sam might have . . . done what he did."

She was quiet long enough that he thought she might have snuck out of the room, but when he turned from the window, she was standing with one hand pushed up into her hair. The robe had come loose, and he could see the curve of her breasts, the slope and smooth skin of her stomach. Her other hand was resting limply against her thigh, palm out, fingers curled up.

"I don't know," she said after a moment, and he knew

immediately that she was lying. "You seem like a nice man, Sheriff. You tell me. What could make a man want to do a thing like that?"

Then she was crying. Her shoulders started to tremble slightly. Her mouth was open but no sound was coming out. Nightingale wanted to go to her, wanted to take her in his arms and assure her that everything was going to come out all right for her in the end, but he didn't. He thought he could forgive her anything if she would tell him the truth. He told himself that it was just because she was beautiful. A beautiful woman could always make you feel helpless.

Delia dropped to the edge of the bed, one hand falling into her lap, her hair hanging over her face like a curtain. He made himself think of the dead man, stretched out at the morgue on a stainless steel slab, and of Sam Holladay, the worn orange prison-issue jumpsuit hanging loosely on his bones. Delia cried hard enough that she couldn't get her breath. When he couldn't bear it anymore, Nightingale walked over and held her shoulders at arm's length and said, "Listen, I don't know what happened. I don't care what happened," but that didn't sound like the right thing to say. He was the sheriff. He patted her arms ridiculously, not wanting to get too close. The next thing he said was out of his mouth before he knew it was coming. He said, "I want to show you something. I want to take you somewhere and show you something."

When she had settled down and gotten dressed, he drove her out to the greyhound farm. He regretted having mentioned it, but it was too late to take the invitation back now. It wasn't time for the dogs to be running, but he flashed his badge and the kennel-keeper was obliging, letting the dogs out of their cages a few at a time. They stood at the fence and watched the dogs racing circles, arching their backs to gather strength, then uncoiling, stretching full length with the effort of running faster. The wind moved Delia's hair.

"I wonder what they think they're chasing," she said. She was calmer now, beginning to sober a little. Her skin was pale as moonlight. "I always thought greyhounds had to be chasing something, like the mechanical rabbit at the track."

"They're chasing something," he said. "Look at them. It's the one thing they know how to do."

Nightingale didn't ask her any more questions. He understood what had happened. It was the oldest story in the world. This is something that could happen in a movie, he thought, the two of us standing here, the dogs tearing through the grass. He drove her home after a little while and turned his attention to other cases, the small misunderstandings that occupied his time in Sherwood. But he didn't stop thinking about her, not entirely. He could go whole days without envisioning her face, but when he closed his eyes to sleep she was there in the place of his criminal dreams, as vivid as a photograph, as real as an actress on a screen, ten times larger than life. The day she left town, a month after her husband was transferred to the federal prison over in Atmore, Nightingale paid Sam Holladay a visit. He found the old man in his cell, lying on the cot with his eyes closed. He swung his legs to the floor when the sheriff entered, made room for him on the cot and the two of them sat there for a few minutes looking at the floor between their shoes. After a while Nightingale said, "She's gone, Sam."

"I know," Holladay said. "I told her I wouldn't see her. She'd waste her life on me. I told the guards not to let her in the visiting room anymore."

Nightingale nodded and linked his fingers together, his

forearms across his knees. He said, "I heard she was moving back to her mother in Mississippi."

"I'm glad," Holladay said.

They sat there for a while longer without speaking, the ward quiet because the rest of the inmates were in the yard. Against the far wall of the cell was a stack of books, history texts mostly. Nightingale guessed that Delia had brought them to keep her husband company. He didn't know, then, that Sam Holladay would be dead in two days, his heart slowing while he slept, coming to a stop sometime around dawn, the coroner said. If he had understood, at that moment, that it was possible for a man to die of a broken heart, he would have thought of something else to say, some way to dispel the quiet between them. But after a few more minutes, he stood and shook Sam Holladay's hand, wished him good luck at a trial that he would never see and called for the guard to lead him back out into the faint, almost breatheable evening.

On his way home, Nightingale drove by the greyhound farm and had the man let Bill out by himself. It was night by then and the dog bolted into the field, then flopped over on his back and wiggled in the grass. Nightingale thought that greyhounds looked funny just acting like dogs, their bodies too lean, almost skeletal, not bred for simple pleasures. He called his name a few times and, to Nightingale's surprise, Bill rolled to his feet, padded over to the fence and sniffed his fingers, his nose cool and damp.

"You're a good dog," he said.

The dog turned and trotted away a few steps then stopped, one forepaw lifted to his chest, and sniffed the heavy air, as if only then realizing that something was out of the ordinary. That it was dark and he was running alone. Nightingale said his name again, softer this time. The dog hesitated, looked in his direction, then started running again, a ghostly blur, sensing that because a man was present, everything must be all right.

Her Divining Rod

Betty Fowler claimed the body. A week had passed since Simon's death with no word about a service, so she called the police and wondered about the status of things. The sheriff asked her a few questions over the phone—Was she aware of a possible relationship between Delia Holladay and the deceased? She told him no. Did she know of any family Simon Bell might have outside of Sherwood? She did not—then he confessed that after all this time, the cadaver was still stretched on a slab in the county morgue. They couldn't find a soul in the world to come down and take it off their hands.

She had surprised herself by lying to the police. Simon, she felt certain, had been sleeping with Delia Holladay. She had watched the two of them coming and going together for more than a month now and why else would Sam Holladay have done such a terrible thing? But what surprised her most was how she felt at the sight of Simon Bell, first on the metal examining table and then in the dark wood coffin and then as they were lowering him into the grave. It was as if she herself had been betrayed.

Besides the minister, Bob Robinson was the only other person at the funeral. In the distance, down the hill, there was another service in progress, with a tent and folding chairs and women in black dresses. Someone was singing. Her chest ached at the thought that Simon could have been in love with another woman. She found it hard to breathe and Robinson noticed her trouble and put an arm around her and asked if she was all right. She waved her handkerchief at him and nodded her okay. She wanted to ask how it was possible for a man to live his life in such a way that the only people to mourn his passing were an old woman and a Yankee from Indiana. When her husband died, she consoled herself with the knowledge that she would never have to feel that sort of pain again. She was too old to be in love. How ridiculous, she thought, to feel this way about a man who could not possibly have shared her sentiment. How foolish to give herself with the expectation of nothing in return. She shook with anger at Simon for making her feel the way she did, though she knew he hadn't done anything to encourage her. She was too old for heartbreak and disappointment, too wise to give her heart, even the smallest part of it, a second time.

In her car after the service, waiting for the air conditioner to cool the interior, she said, "You goddam motherfucker. You pansy-ass dickhead," and then she was laughing. She could see his brow wrinkling in surprise, his eyes widening at her progress in the field of profanity.

Bob Robinson leaned against her door.

He said, "Did you just say what I think you said?"

"Fuck you, Bob Robinson," she said. "Thanks for coming."

He smiled and patted the doorframe. "Fuck you, too, Mrs. Fowler. I know he would appreciate what you did for him today." He rapped the window with his knuckle and walked off toward his car.

At home, she made a pitcher of iced tea and took a glass out to the sleeping porch. She could see the house, just across the curve in the road. The door closed, the curtains drawn. To keep herself from getting too gloomy, Betty Fowler went inside and retrieved her divining rod from the umbrella stand in the entry hall. She made her way across the street to look for the gold her husband had left behind. For a long time, she stood in the dead center of the sixteenth fairway with her eyes closed. Insects chattered resolutely in the grass, sunlight pressed on her clothes. Once she heard a golf cart passing on the path, the murmur of voices, but for the most part the course was empty. After a while, she heard a muffled thump and opened her eyes to see a golf ball rolling toward her across the grass, but she didn't see anyone at the tee. The ball rolled to a stop at her feet, and she stooped to pick it up. It was grass-stained and chipped, the twine showing through in places. She heard a little girl's voice yell, "You crazy old bitch."

It had been a week, at least, since she'd been accosted by the girl. She paused a moment, considering her reply. She had been waiting for this. At that instant, as though visited by a revelation, the identity of the girl came to her. She let the end of the divining rod touch the ground and rested her weight on it like a cane.

"Is that you Maddie Robinson?" she said. "You've got about ten seconds to show yourself. Or I'm calling your father at work."

No answer. She said, "I just saw your daddy this morning, so don't think for a minute that I'm bluffing. I'm gonna start counting now." But before she could begin, Maddie came out from behind the trees, her eyes on the ground, her hands clasped at her middle. She was barefoot, her toes curled sheepishly into the grass. Betty Fowler said, "Come over here. I wanna know who taught you to talk to me like that."

Maddie crept over and said, "My brother taught me. I heard my Dad say some of those things, too."

"Un-hunh," Betty Fowler said.

She couldn't help liking the girl. The way her cheeks blossomed red with embarrassment, her hair making a cowlick at the crown of her head. Her knees dotted with scabs, her nails chewed to the quick.

"You're not the only one with a nasty mouth," she said, drawing a breath. "Goddam motherfucking bitch ass queer. See there. Simon Bell taught me."

Maddie looked at her, amazed. In a quiet voice, she said, "He's dead."

She didn't know what to say. Her chest went tight. Maddie's eyes were a mix of fear and expectation. The girl was so young. She thought she should tell her something about life and death, about the persistent way of the world. The way lives could reflect one another, forward and backward through time, like sunlight on broken glass. But she stopped herself. Instead, she said, "Know what I do out here all day, Maddie?"

"My brother told me you were a witch."

Betty Fowler laughed, softly. "I'm not a witch. I'm divining for gold. You know what that means? It's a kind of magic, I guess. Would you like to learn?"

Maddie nodded, her mouth open with surprise. Betty Fowler handed her the divining rod, showed her how to hold it properly, told her what it might feel like when she found the gold. She reached around the girl and covered her hands with her own. She could smell the summer in her hair, could feel the warmth of summers past in her skin. They walked together for a few steps, then Betty Fowler opened her arms and let Maddie move away. The girl kept her eyes closed tight. She said, "Mrs. Fowler, are you still there? Am I doing right?"

"I'm here, baby," she said. "You're doing fine."

· A NOTE ON THE TYPE ·

The typeface used in this book is a version of Palatino, origi-
nally designed in 1950 by Hermann Zapf (b. 1918), one of the
most prolific contemporary type designers, who has also cre-
ated Melior and Optima. Palatino was first used to set the in-
troduction of a book of Zapf's hand lettering, in an edition of
eighty copies on Japan paper handbound by his wife, Gu-
drun von Hesse; the book sold out quickly and Zapf's name
was made. (Remarkably, the lettering had actually been done
when the self-taught calligrapher was only twenty-one.) Intended mainly for "display" (title pages, headings), Palatino
owes its appearance both to calligraphy and the requirements
of the cheap German paper at the time—perhaps why it is
also one of the best-looking fonts on low-end computer print-
ers. It was soon used to set text, however, causing Zapf to re-
draw its more elaborate letters.